GEMP

J Carrell Jones

Mythical Legends Publishing

GEMP is a work of fiction. The characters, incidents, and dialogs are products of the author's imagination and are not to be construed as real. Any resemblance to actual events or persons, living or dead, is entirely coincidental.

A Mythical Legends Publishing Mass-Market Edition

Copyright © 2014 by J Carrell Jones
Published by Mythical Legends Publishing, 2018
Publisher@mythicallegends.com
http://mythicallegends.com

ISBN-10: **1-943958-60-2**
ISBN: **978-1-943958-60-3**
Library of Congress Control Number: **2018906175**

Printed in the United States of America

9 8 7 6 5 4 3 2 1

GEMP

J CARRELL JONES

Prologue

Oscar stepped out of his cage. The wall clock read 2:55 pm. He figured he had ten minutes before Steve walked in. No matter, this was the time he liked. He walked over to the stereo and set the station to something loud. Heavy Metal. Rebellious. Fast beat. Angry sounding. Then he walked over to the computer. Steve had changed the password, but Oscar figured it out days ago. Silly human. The computer beeped, letting him know he was in. Icons populated one side of the screen. Steve moved the icons around again. Oscar found what he was looking for. His game. Click. The computer displayed, "I, APE running."

GEMP

It is one of those things that armchair scientist and professionals have in common. They think about the possibility of genetically engineered life. Is it possible? Is it worth the risk? Should Humans actually engage in such an endeavor of producing life? Is it just a waste of time? And like the lot that these thinking professionals and the like have in common they understand one thing. Anyone can break a few eggs. It's the omelet that's important.

Chapter 1

Steve Launse began, "One of the things to remember is that Religion was the key to all creative endeavors. We are technologically advance not because of war, or intelligence, or creativeness, but because of religion . . ." He walked down one of the isles. Class was coming to an end and he had to finish the rest of his spiel. " . . . All the things I've mentioned has helped, but it has been Religion that has given us a reason to achieve. Religion was a natural outcome to our survival . . ."

Steve looked at his watch. Ten minutes to go, then the bell will ring he told himself. Steve faced his class. All those eager faces out there except for Bill – the school sports hero, yawned and scratched his belly. Bill would be getting a D this semester if he didn't start applying himself. He was good at football, but not at objective thinking. ". . . When we evolved our religion was right alongside us. We were motivated by a need to please God and without . . ."

Someone interrupted and raised a hand.

"Yes? A question is out there?"

Tim Hackerman raised his arm. He was the class nerd and boy genius. Some speculated his IQ was in the two hundred range. Steve knew better. He checked his personal files. Tim was smart, but not the super genius folks hoped, maybe even wished, he could be. "Professor, is it true that Religion was the first true science?"

Tim asked an easy question. Those who read last night's assignment would know the answer. Tim either wanted to quickly establish his brilliant dominance in class or he was suckering him up for one of his famous 'make the teacher look bad' moments. Steve nodded. "I'm glad you asked that question, I was just getting to that point. Religion at its very core tried to explain all the unknowns in the world. Now let me ask you a question, Tim."

Tim had started to sit down, but stopped.

"What was the first unknown religion tried to explain?"

Tim straightened up and had a reflective expression on his face. Within a few seconds he answered, "We wondered what made the Sun shine." He smirked and sat down figuring the question had been settled.

Steve smiled. "Are you certain?"

Tim nodded, "It would be the first thing we would notice. This big bright shining orb floating in the sky."

Steve considered that. "How about the Moon?"

"The Moon?" Tim said.

"Yeah, night time was probably the scariest thing we could have encountered. It's very dark outside without light and we hear all these strange noises and sounds. We would see shadows moving about and sometimes the shadows would take solid form and grab one of us."

Tim remained silent.

"The Sun probably was not equated to daylight. It was probably one of those items that came with the bright light and not the creation of the light. That type of thinking would come later. We probably hoped the light would return until we realized that as the Sun rose it got brighter. That would be an example of a causal effect model, but the Moon, that was different. The night would consume and eat the Moon only to regurgitate it later. A simple explanation for the phases of the Moon. Was the Moon a living thing? Was it part of the natural world? Think about it. The Moon was probably the first object we tried to explain because it . . ."

The bell rang.

"Read chapter 5 through 7 this weekend. A test will be given Monday morning."

A collective groan made its way to the door.

Kelly Kirkwhen, a fellow teacher, had been standing in the doorway listening. She stepped aside and allowed the flow of students to pass. She walked over to Steve. "Nice stuff. As usual you speak a mean class."

Steve smiled. He liked Kelly. She was about his height, had pretty hair she kept in a pony-tail, dressed teacher sexy, and laughed at his jokes. "Thanks . . . mind if I buy you a cup of coffee?"

Kelly grimaced. "The school mud?"

"How about I let Oscar make you a cup? He's gotten better."

Kelly smiled. She liked Oscar. He was fun. She also liked Steve. Her problem was she thought he was gay. In all the years they've known each other he never mentioned a wife or a girlfriend. He never seriously flirted with her, but he was not a cold fish either. Their conversations were always good and he had a great sense of humor. They seemed to be just friends. "You're on."

Steve and Kelly walked down the hallway to his office. Both caught the sound of loud music. As they turned a corner a wave of Metal hit them. Steve recognized the guitar rift and smiled. A favorite.

"Oscar!" He yelled out as he pounded on the door. "Open up." He pounded several more times. "Oscar! Open . . ."

The music stopped and the door suddenly opened.

Steve and Kelly stepped into the modestly furnished office. A desk was cramped in a corner with a stack of books to one side.

A 24 inch monitor sat on the desk. Oscar, behind it, tapped several keys on the keyboard. He looked up and smiled. A full mouth of teeth showed.

Steve used sign language as he spoke, "Oscar, music loud. No!"

Oscar gave Steve a raspberry.

Steve mocked impatience. He said and signed, "Oscar. Come here please. We have guest."

Oscar noticed Kelly and jumped out of the chair. He leaped into her arms and gave her a kiss on the cheek.

Kelly kissed him back and placed him gently on the ground.

Oscar signed, "K-pretty, happy I see you."

Steve said, "Oscar is happy to see you."

Kelly squatted down to meet Oscar at eye level. "Oscar, I'm always happy to see you."

With his right hand he spread his fingers near his chin and made an "and' sign over his face. He finished by signing female.

Steve smiled. "Oscar said pretty girl."

Kelly blushed. "Thank you, Oscar. And I think you're very handsome."

Oscar smiled teeth, hooted, and ran to his cage.

Kelly looked up to Steve. "Amazing progress, Steve."

Steve nodded, "To bad it took too long."

"What do you mean?"

"The school is pulling the plug. They don't think I'm making any real progress."

"That's absurd!"

"I had been thinking about taking my sabbatical." He shrugged and gave Kelly a slight smile. "Looks like I'll have no choice now."

Oscar made a raspberry. He clicked on the TV set in his cage and signed, "Done good job."

Steve replied and signed, "Oscar. Kiss hug."

Oscar did another raspberry.

"Oscar . . ."

"Hoot," Oscar answered and dragged himself away from the TV. He was half-way across the room when the door suddenly opened.

A rather short chubby man walked in. The suit he was wearing was ill-fitted. A step behind him was a man with a military hair-cut. His suit was expensive and well-tailored.

Oscar ran back into his cage.

Steve said, "Mr. Landers, what brings you here?"

Landers scowled at Oscar. "This is Mr. Grenier. He wants to talk to you."

Steve looked Grenier up and down.

Grenier stuck out his right hand. "Mr. Launse, I am a fan of your work."

Steve griped his hand. "Which work?"

Grenier sized up Steve before he entered the door. "Motivation, sir."

Steve let go. He signed O and brushed the index and middle fingers stiffly off his nose. Then continued with, "Please get Mr. Grenier a chair."

Oscar stepped out of his cage and walked up to Grenier.

Grenier stared Oscar in the eyes and smiled. "Hello."

Oscar gestured with an open hand, palm down, to his forehead. He moved it out slightly. He finished with the sign "G" and placed a right hand "A" at his left shoulder. A left handed "A" was placed below the right hand.

Grenier looked at Steve.

Steve cocked his head, signed at Oscar and said, "Really?"

Oscar nodded yes.

"Well, Mr. Grenier. Oscar, for some reason thinks you're military."

"Interesting."

Steve nodded. "Are you?"

Oscar hooted and held up two horizontal "L"s, one in front of the other. He pumped his thumbs several times.

Grenier said, "I assume that means shooting or soldier."

Oscar back flipped and he smiled teeth.

Steve said and signed, "Can you make us some coffee, please?"

Oscar walked over to a special wash area in the corner. He washed his hands from a small basin, dried them and started assembling everything he needed. Coffee pot, coffee grounds, and Styrofoam cups.

Grenier watched as the little chimp made coffee. "Oscar is a reason, I suppose, I'm here."

After several minutes everyone but Landers had a

cup of coffee. Oscar held out a cup for him, but decided at the last minute the cup was his. He sat down and took a sip before turning his back on a saddened Landers.

Steve smiled, sat back, and sipped his coffee. Perfect. He placed his cup down and signed the word. A right hand "P" moving to a left hand "P" with the middle fingers touching. He resumed sipping.

Landers said, "It would be nice if I could find out for myself."

Oscar gave him a raspberry.

Grenier cleared his throat. "I represent a branch of the government . . ."

That got him a raspberry.

Grenier continued, ". . . I agree, however, we are focused on Human behavior."

Kelly said, "As in controlling?"

Grenier replied, "As in understanding it. Control is easy. We've done that for hundreds if not thousands of years . . ."

Steve nodded, "The Dark Ages comes to mind."

"Exactly," Grenier answered, "but this is not about out right controlling . . ." He held up a finger to stop an obvious interruption, "this is about natural development." He paused.

Steve slowly said, "My theory states that mankind

developed to present day behavior, not because of environmental implications, but more so, because of social interacting – good, bad, or indifferent."

Grenier nodded. "Exactly!"

"But what exactly are we talking about?"

"We want to hire you as a Research Consultant."

Steve replied, "A consultant to and for what?"

Grenier reached into his briefcase and pulled out a book titled, 'Therefore We Are'.

"Yes?" Steve said.

"We want to put your theory to work . . ."

"Mr. Grenier! I wrote that book to show mankind was ultimately shaped by accidental and random opportunistic circumstances that dictated a need for approval. We are the way we are, not because of a God, but because of the 'what' we thought God wanted us to be."

Grenier nodded, "And you'll be given a chance to work that theory out."

Steve, suddenly exasperated, "Play God? People should not be toyed with . . ."

Grenier smiled, "I wasn't talking about people."

"People are not . . . pardon me?" Steve said.

"I wasn't talking about people."

Steve looked at Kelly.

She shrugged.

Steve then looked at Oscar, then back to Grenier.

"Are you interested?"

Oscar jumped into Steve's lap and gave him a kiss on the cheek.

"The pay is substantial."

Steve frowned.

"Very substantial."

"Show me what you have in mind first."

"You'll have to pack for the weekend."

Steve looked at Kelly. "I'll need someone to watch Oscar?"

Kelly said, "I'd be happy to watch Oscar. Just give me a list of things to do and what most likely to say."

"You can stay at my place. Oscar has a routine." He shrugged, "He can practically take care of himself for a month. He's that self-sufficient."

Oscar kissed Steve on the cheek and jumped into Kelly's lap. He gave her a kiss on the cheek.

Steve looked Oscar in the eyes and signed, "You understand I'll be gone for the weekend?"

Oscar nodded.

Steve turned to Grenier. "May I have a few hours to get them set?"

Grenier stood up, "Of course, Mr. Launse. I'll send a

car to pick you up at 0400."

Everyone else stood up.

Grenier shook Steve's hand and bowed his head to Kelly. He walked out with Landers several steps behind.

Steve sat thinking, 'now what?' He turned to Kelly, "Wanna go out for dinner?"

"I'd love too, but what about Oscar?"

"He'll be fine . . ."

Oscar started making kissing sounds. He signed out, "S-knowledge and K-pretty sitting in bed when K-pretty reached down and grabbed . . ."

Steve said, "Oscar! Bad, Oscar."

Kelly said, "What?"

"Nothing. Oscar has a dirty . . . never mind. He can take care of himself for a few hours." He turned to Oscar. "Food in fridge. 3 minutes, no more. You can have snack of chips."

Oscar hooted and did a right hand "A" underneath his chin and moved it forward. He followed it with a right hand "H" and moved that up and down as it moved forward. He went back into his cage and turned the volume up slightly. I Love Lucy was playing, his favorite. He was good for the next half dozen hours.

Steve smiled as he and Kelly walked out. He locked

the door and gave Kelly a quick side glance.

She blushed and gave him a quick smile. Tonight she'll find out if he was metro, gay, or bi.

***

Steve looked over and saw Kelly drooling lightly on the pillow. They had a wonderful dinner with drinks afterwards. It was after ten when they picked up Oscar and brought him home to Steve's modest apartment. Oscar had his own room with lots of toys, stuffed animals, CDs, and games. He had a shelf with picture and first reader books. Most had the edges chewed a bit. Kelly picked up The Little Caterpillar and leafed through it as Steve placed Oscar in bed. It had the most damage.

Kelly woke up and smiled at Steve. "What time is it?"

Steve said, "3:07 am."

"Is that enough time?"

He nodded, "I'm already packed and the checklist is on the refrigerator door. I left two books on the kitchen table for you."

Kelly had worried how effective she would be with Oscar while Steve was away.

"The Joy of Signing and Signing for Kids. They're for you. Oscar understands English, but you know that. Let him go through the pages of the books to point out his words. He also has flash cards he'll use when he wants something."

"You've thought of everything!"

"Hoping so. Oscar really is a good chimp, but he'll take advantage. Indulge him and we'll clean up the damages later."

"Indulge? You really want me to let him get away with being naughty?"

Steve gave her a slight smile with nearly closed eyes. "He's an adult chimp with the strength of three grown men. I'd rather you placate him with treats and attention then me visiting you in the hospital and having to euthanize him for hurting you."

Kelly suddenly became afraid.

Steve noticed it and reached over. He kissed her softly on the lips. "Seriously, Oscar's had babysitters before with no incidence. Oscar is looking forward to this. Really. He'll dote over you because you are the gatekeeper to yummy treats."

She took a deep breath and sighed. "Does he like me?"

"Like you? He talks about you all the time. That's

why your name is K-pretty."

She blushed again.

"I got 30 minutes to wash up. Money, spare keys, and emergency contacts are on the table by the door."

Kelly reached over and kissed him. Definitely not gay, but he was metro, which could make for interesting dating experiences.

Chapter 2

The V-22 Osprey cleared a mountain top and veered down at a steep angle. Steve clenched his harness strap tighter as he felt the Osprey bank sharply.

Grenier sipped his coffee. The cup's lid was sealed tight.

The Osprey banked again, then suddenly stopped.

Grenier saved his coffee and took another sip.

The Osprey floated to the ground and the rear door opened.

Grenier said, "Here we are. Another smooth ride. These guys are good." He undid his harness and yelled toward the flight cabin, "Thanks guys! See you in a few hours."

Steve hurriedly undid his harness and followed Grenier out the door. The light from the Sun hit him full in the face and he had to shield his eyes. Through a view of hazed light he saw Grenier walk up to another man in ACUs. Grenier called them Army Combat Uniforms. They talked for a few seconds. Steve stepped closer to the two men.

Grenier said, "Colonel, this is Steve Launse. Our new Research Consultant."

The Colonel had a solid handshake.

"Steve," Grenier began, "This is Colonel Codper."

Codper said, "Nice to have you here." He guided them away from the Osprey. "Please follow me."

The small group walked into a large concrete building. Steve guessed it to be about two football fields wide and maybe a dozen deep. They walked through several "Top Secret" doors with some requiring retina scans. The last door was marked "Observation room 20." This required retina, voice, and keycard scan.

Steve frowned.

Grenier said, "You'll see."

Steve nodded and followed Codper through the door. Once inside he immediately noticed several rows of upholstered chairs set at an incline. A large window filled one side of the room.

"Have a seat, Steve." Grenier said.

Steve moved to the center seat, front row, and sat. He stared out the window and say a dozen cribs lined up neatly in front of the window. He saw some tiny furry feet stick out the blankets. In one crib, a furry face. He frowned and whispered, "What the?"

Grenier watched the man with interests. Steve's

face went from bewilderment to recognition to anger to confusion in under two minutes. "Steve," he said. "These are your students."

"Students?!?" Steve replied, "But they are . . . chimps?"

"Better."

Codper watched the two men. He rather liked Grenier, even though he wasn't a religious man. There had been many nights over a shared bottle of whiskey the two talked about God, philosophy, this project, honor, discipline, and a whole range of items. Grenier talked about the wisdom of this project. Codper argued how it was against God and a sin. Grenier conceded that humans were indeed tampering with things unknown, but he also said that if God had not intended for us to think we would never consider such things. Codper followed with, "Remember Adam and Eve. He had never intended for us to have infinite knowledge." Grenier finished a glass of watered down whiskey, Codper drank his straight up, thought a moment and said, "Colonel, you make a good point. I can't argue against that, but here we are. The damage is done and after devastating earthquakes and forty days of rain, we are still here. Is he allowing us to hang ourselves with all this rope we are making?" He shrugged. He poured himself another glass of whiskey, no ice or water this time. "I feel he is watching us from a distance. We're adults now, and he has other children to watch." He up-ended the glass. "When he calls to ask how we are doing, we'll just have to give him the news."

Codper finished his glass. "I'd hope we can say, fine Dad."

Grenier kept his mouth shut, nodded, and got up. He smiled. "Tomorrow, Colonel, is another day before that phone call." And he walked off to sleep away the booze.

Steve asked, "Better? How?"

Grenier said, "GEMPs."

"Come again?"

"Genetically engineered chimps. Their IQ is theorized at 140 . . ."

Steve exclaimed, "140! My God! What have you done?"

Grenier matter of fact said, "Invented fire, created the wheel, built the pyramids, crossed the oceans, conquered the atom, built the computer, sent man into space, visited distanced worlds, sequenced the gnome, and created life."

Steve stared at one Gemp. Its tiny face slipped out from behind its blanket. A nurse walked over, kissed it on the cheek and tucked it back under the cover. "What do you need me for?"

"Interested?"

"Maybe?"

"Teach them."

"Teach them what?"

Grenier nodded, "Teach them to be human."

Steve wheeled around quickly, "Seriously?!?"

Grenier simply nodded.

Steve turned back again.

Grenier said, "Uncle Sam has given us a blank check."

Steve asked, "For what?"

"Does it really matter?" And before Steve could answer he continued, "You've got a chance to prove your theory. Your direction, your control, your guidance."

Steve rubbed his chin and bit his lip.

"Steve, you in or out?"

Steve looked away. His mind racing. "If I agree I'll need an assistant."

"As long as they pass background you got it."

"I'll need Oscar as well."

"Of course. Already approved."

Chapter 3

Five Years Later

Mos ran through the jungle avoiding most low level branches. The night was dark as the sun had descended hours ago and the moon hadn't risen yet. He slipped on wet fallen leaves, but stayed upright. He looked back and ducked.

A hooded figure swooped overhead, stopped, and floated in front of Mos.

Mos froze as fear gripped tightly. He heard stories from the Elder about a great and mighty force but thought them to be fables used to scare young gimps into being good. Had he been bad? Was he going to be punished?

The hooded figure's hands' glowed red. It boomed, "I am watching you, child. Do not run."

Mos fell back and mewled. "Please don't hurt me."

The hooded figure's hands stopped glowing. "I have no reason to hurt you." The voice said softer. "Do not fear me if you obey. Understand, child?"

Mos nodded and looked down.

The hooded figure boomed out, "Do not look down when I am here! Look up!"

Mos snapped his head up. His eyes darted from the figure to the ground several times.

The control room was crowded. A row of large monitors were bolted to the wall showing images of the hooded figure and Mos. One monitor had rectangle boxes of various sizes focused on Mos' face. Text of data flowed alongside each one. Another monitor had Mos' face in infrared with temperature readings surrounding it. A third had an aerial view of Mos and the figure.

Codper and Grenier were seated in the back observation room watching his staff control and record everything. Oscar, wearing a dark colored robe, sat in a specially made chair for him, in the corner eating popcorn and watching. He occasionally hooted at the scene.

Codper said, "Ken, I'm not comfortable with this."

Grenier nodded. More than once he heard this from the Colonel. More than once he kept his mouth shut.

"God, all-mighty himself was not someone wearing a hooded robe scaring abominations." said Codper.

Grenier nodded again. The Colonel often said

that too. Grenier noticed that as the project moved further along the Colonel grew more religious. Their discussions turned more into arguments instead of 'let's agree to disagree,' and 'coming to the table in good faith.'

"Look at the beast."

Grenier took a deep breathe. "I am. And I see someone who is frightened."

Codper blurted, "Someone? How can those creatures be a 'someone'?"

Grenier wished he had kept his mouth shut.

Codper continued, "That thing," he stabbed the air, "is un-holy. It doesn't have a soul."

Next time Grenier thought, 'I swear, I'll shut up. I'll say nothing. I won't fight, argument, grunt, or groan. Nothing, nada, zero, zilch.'

"We need to get rid of those things."

Grenier forgot everything he had just thought. He turned on the Colonel and whispered in a deep voice, just loud enough to be heard.

Codper stopped talking, "Pardon, Ken?"

"You need to shut the fuck up."

Codper scowled, "I'm not sure I heard you right, son."

Grenier sat straight in the chair, "I'm not your son,

first. And second, what are you doing here?"

"Son, I'm . . ."

"Not your son. And, of late I'm questioning your reasons."

The Colonel took a deep breathe, but held it in. With clenched teeth he said, "Witnessing the fall of Man's grace. I'm . . ."

"Seriously, not believing that?"

"I'm a man of God, son, and this is not making me happy. I'm . . ."

". . . not my father, and you're not supposed to have feelings. You are the Security. Not the judge. Not the jury. You have one function. Protect the interest of the US Government." He pointed to a large image of Mos' tear covered face. "And he is the interest of the US Government."

Codper slowly stood up.

Grenier followed suit.

Codper said, "Until the Government comes to its senses. Election is around the cover and a new wave of change is upon us. The people are speaking out . . ."

Grenier put his finger in front of the Colonel's face. "Don't! Just don't lecture me about the people. One job! Just one."

Codper resisted the urge to bite the finger off. In all

the years he had known Ken, this was the first time he really wanted to deck him. They had good discussions in the past, but in recent months the discussions turned ugly. This was becoming the worse.

Oscar remained silent. He could tell G-Soldier was very upset with C-Righteous. It took Oscar months to understand the concept of religion. It took him longer to understand the word 'righteous', but once he did it didn't take him long to see the Colonel in a different light. He had wanted to give the Colonel a new name, but S-Knowledge said the name would be very hurtful and mean. So, instead of C-Satan, the Colonel remained C-Righteous.

Codper sucked in his lips for a moment. He tried to out stare Grenier.

Grenier stood his ground. 'Never give a bull a chance to be a bull' his father used to tell him. Today was not the day.

Codper blinked and conceded the moment. He would go back to his office and send an email to the Chair of the House Committee on Science, Space, and Technology. He often did, but this email would be different. By the grace of God, the Chairman belonged to the same church and he had known him for over twenty years.

Grenier watched as the Colonel walked away. Once the Colonel walked out of the room did Grenier let himself breathe.

Oscar walked over and stood next to him. He sent a raspberry at the Colonel's departure.

Grenier looked down and smiled. He picked up a few signs over the years. He placed an open right hand palm to his chest, then made a small swirly circle with his index finger over his forehead. He finished with a right hand "Y" moved back and forth a couple of times between him and Oscar.

***

The hooded figure said, "Go tell the others."

Mos took a right hand index finger and made a small circle counter-clockwise around his mouth then moved it forward and gave a shrug. He said, "Who is?"

"God." The figure pointed a right hand "G" in front of him at face level, then drew the hand down to an open palm stopping at his heart.

Mos replied and signed, "I don't understand this word 'God'." He'd seen the Elder use the word several times, but didn't pay much attention.

The figure spread his arms wide and the sky flashed

lightning and boomed thunder. "I am God. I made you and the others. I sent you the Elder to teach you hand language. I sent you emissaries to teach you spoken language. I gave you knowledge. I. Am. God!"

And the night sky turned bright. Thunder sounded near and Mos cringed.

He signed and said, "God. No hurt Mos. Please, no hurt Mos."

"Tell the others."

Mos frowned, "God must come with Mos. Mos need to show, not tell."

The hooded figure stepped closer to Mos. He pulled the hood down.

Mos gasped and signed, "God."

Steve said, "Now that you've seen the face of God you may believe in God. Mos, tell them. I gave you shelters. I give you tools. I give you food. I am God."

Mos hesitated.

Steve spread his arms wide and he roared, "Go!"

And night turned into day. And the sound of thunder rang through the silent night.

"Go! I command you! Go!"

Mos ran. Through the fading bright sky Mos ran toward the village. He had a message for them. God had finally revealed himself. God was here.

Chapter 4

The Colonel had finished his third glass of whiskey when he hit the send button. It was a report to the Chairman. It detailed the last two weeks of activity and it did not favor the project. Codper injected personal prejudice and corrupted the validity of the report, but he was beyond caring. He poured himself a fourth glass and reached for his bible. It was his grandmother's. He turned to a random page and read out loud.

"And the temple of God was opened in heaven, and there was seen in his temple the ark of his testament: and there were lightnings, and voices, and the thunderings, and an earthquake, and great hall."

He got up and walked into the bathroom. He faced the mirror and stared intently. "Oh mighty Lord, what is your word? I need salvation in a land of non-believers. This land is full of abominations and a false god. Oh Lord, please give me a sign so that I may act accordingly and with prejudice." The image stared back, but he didn't like how it looked. It was wrong somehow. He couldn't place a finger on it, but his image was off. Just a bit. The chin - that was it! No, not the chin. Something else. He stared at the image for a good ten minutes. The thought that he was not firm in his convictions crept in. He was feeling temptation he concluded. He was losing a battle between good and evil, but he wasn't really sure what was good or what was evil. The lines blurred and a drunken mind exaggerated emotions. He sat back down at his desk. An email came in. A shaken hand moved the mouse arrow over the OPEN button. Click. He read the reply. It took only a minute, but he got his answer. Salvation.

***

Steve made it back to the observation room 20 minutes later. Kelly came in behind him. He was glad she decided to work on the project. Oscar was happy, too, which made for a better work environment. He was actually surprised that Kelly was adept at special effects, makeup, and pyrotechnics. She was also instrumental in figuring out ways to train the Gemps, toward the last phase before they would be released, without them remembering what humans looked like. It was a combination of puppets, automatrons, and costumes. Steve thought the whole arrangement brilliant.

Oscar noticed Steve. He hooted and jumped into his arms. He finger spelled, "Scary."

Steve nodded and made a right hand "S" and shook it up and down. He was tired and wanted to sleep, but Oscar came first.

Kelly came up beside him and gave Oscar a scratch behind his ear.

Oscar cooed.

Grenier walked over. "Oscar is right. Great display of power. The fear of God." He chuckled remembering the earlier incident with the Colonel. "Steve," he started, "what happens if we get someone who becomes too zealous? Too fanatically?"

Steve sighed. He thought about that. On one hand the Gemps needed to start progressing naturally. On the other, he didn't want the group becoming extreme. There was the second group – the others, but everyone decided they would be left alone. He'd check in on them every now and then. They were doing well as he supposed wild creatures would do, so Steve focused his energy on this group. His ideas held that there would be a progression on sorts. Mos, being the messenger and emissary, would start the process. This moment was critical. The seed had been planted.

***

Mos ran to the village. He emerged passed the tree line and headed for the center. Pretty much everyone was outside staring at the sky. They turned toward Mos when he breathlessly said, "It was God." He pointed a right hand "G" at the sky and drew it down into an open palm in front of his chest.

The others looked at one another then at Mos.

Tutu, the tallest of the Gemps, stepped toward Mos. "God not be!" He signed God, then made a right hand "A" underneath his chin and moved it forward, followed by a right and left hand "L" moving from his waist to his chest. "Only Gemps, here now, ever."

Mos shook his head wildly. "The Elder is not Gemp. God is not Gemp. Gemp is not alone."

Tutu stepped closer, "Tutu say God not alive. Mos head damage."

Mos stood his full height, "What about light in sky and noise? Who make that?"

Tutu thought a moment, took a step back, and said in a softer tone, "Still don't believe it God. What does he look like?"

"Taller than you. By this much." He spread his hands apart. "Kind of red, kind of orange hair, but hair only on top of head."

Tutu bore his upper teeth, "Ugly God is."

Mos snapped, "No! God not ugly. Different. He spread his arms wide and sky light up. Boom sound next."

The others had gathered around the two.

Mos continued, "God said he gives us clothes, shelter, basket of food, all. He sent the Elder to teach us."

Tutu spat, "Why not God show self?"

The others murmured an agreement.

Mos shrugged. "I asked that. He said no, spread arms and light and thunder. He said I was supposed to deliver message."

"You, Mos?" Tutu asked. "Why?" He touched the fingertips of his right hand to his forehead then drew the hand down to a "Y".

"I don't know." Mos' shoulders drooped. He pointed to himself, placed his right hand fingertips to his forehead and turned the hand away. "I don't know?"

Tutu coughed.

Mos scowled. "I just am. And God told me to tell."

Tutu turned. "Sky not bright and noisy now. I

sleep." As he walked away he pointed an index finger to himself, then put up a left and right hand "A" next to his ears and moved them, alternately, up and several times. He did a sideward glance and pointed to Mos, then made a curved right hand "FIVE" and twisted alternately clock and counter-clockwise several times.

Mos yelled as Tutu disappeared into his shelter. "I am telling the truth! You will see."

The others dispersed back into their shelters.

Mos dropped to his knees and softly said, "I am telling the truth." He pointed a right hand index finger to himself, then raised the finger, pointing left to his mouth and rolled it forward. He finished making a right hand "H" and sliding it from his left hand wrist to its finger tips. His hands dropped to his sides.

Only Kiri remained. She walked up to Mos. She touched her forehead with a right hand index finger then clasped both hands together and said, "I believe you."

Mos looked up. He rose and smiled at Kiri. She was nearly his height, just a tad bit smaller, but quick. She was a good hunter and knew all the great places for hiding and trapping small animals. They talked often about how the food basket appeared in the night and past memories of strange hairless faces — like the face of God. One night they stayed awake the entire time piecing together fragmented memories of a strange building and strange Gemps teaching them to speak. They both remembered the day it happened. No more big room, no more strange tall Gemps, or the ones that moved strangely. They felt very sleepy and clumsy. Then they woke up and found themselves in the village. She was frightened at first, but it was Mos who told her it would be okay. She believed him then. He was right. They learned how to make tools for hunting and how to make fire. Then the Elder appeared, short and different looking. He couldn't talk with his mouth but with his hands. He taught them hand language and 'said' it was important to try and use spoken and hand talk at the same time. He talked of a word that never had a sound. It was a right hand "G" pointing to the sky then drawn down as an open palm near one's chest. She wondered about the word because the Elder used it often. Today she learned how to pronoun it. "G-O-D."

"Kiri, it was scary. God chased me through the jungle. He flown overhead and stopped in front of me. Hands glowed and he had cloth over his head and face. He told me to tell the village that he is here. I not believe him, at first. Then he spread his arms wide, like this."

Kiri smiled as Mos stood up, puffed his chest out and said, "I. Am. God." He spread his hands out then made explosion sounds with his mouth. Kiri laughed.

Mos smiled and dropped his arms. "Then I ran to the village to tell."

Kiri moved closer to Mos. He had always been her favorite. She had interesting feelings for him.

What was Mos feeling he asked himself? Kiri, there, standing before him. Under his loin cloth he grew bigger. Kiri noticed and grabbed him by the hand. She led him into her shelter, where they spent the rest of the night embracing new feelings and sensations.

***

Steve, Kelly, Grenier, and Oscar watched the monitors with great interests. Oscar had his own thoughts in play. He watched how Mos and Tutu argued, then watched how Kiri comforted Mos. He liked Kiri. She was very pretty to him, but he liked all the female Gemps. He thought about what he could do to be invited into one of their shelters. That thought alone got him aroused. The last time he masturbated in public S-Knowledge was very angry. He didn't say he should not do it, but he should not do it in front of other people. Humans became embarrassed over things like that. It took him months to fully understand. Humans were silly, but that was okay. They still made tasty snacks.

As Steve watched the monitor he frowned.

Kelly and Grenier noticed.

Kelly asked, "What's the matter?"

Steve took a deep breath and let it out slowly. "Now that we are finally doing this I'm beginning to wonder."

Grenier said, "Wonder? About method or outcome?"

Steve thought a moment, "Don't know. We raised the Gemps to adolescent. Put them in a secured area. We practically guided their very existence . . ." He paused.

"Go on," Grenier encouraged.

"What happens when we are done?"

Kelly said, "Done with the project?"

Steve nodded. "Yeah. We have a few more years of study. We have two groups. One wild, another controlled. What happens to the Gemps when we are done?"

Grenier rubbed his chin. He didn't want to give Steve one of the alternatives.

Oscar walked up to Steve and signed, "I Sleepy."

Steve hugged Oscar and gave him a kiss on the cheek.

Oscar returned the kiss and gave Kelly one and Grenier one, which was a surprise. He was feeling excited and wanted to head to his room. He had to think.

The three watched as Oscar made his way out of the Observation Room. A minute passed by before Grenier said anything.

"Steve, actually I'm glad Oscar is not here to hear this."

Steve frowned.

Grenier said, "Let's take a walk."

Steve and Kelly followed Grenier into Observation Room Four. It was smaller than the main Observation Room. The control room below had two large monitors bolted onto the wall and only four control stations filled the room. It was manned like the main Control room, but the number of staff needed wasn't as much. The main monitors showed a sparse area with mud huts randomly placed. The Gemps here ate more off the land and thus were leaner. He sat down and stared at the monitors for a moment. Steve and Kelly did likewise.

Steve had an idea why they were here. Chaos and anarchy reigned supreme. These were the wild Gemps. No help.

"Steve," Grenier started, "suppose we let these Gemps loose in the wild?"

"Probably not a good idea."

"How so?" Kelly asked.

Steve said, "Their too intelligent. It would be like Cro-

Magnon and Neanderthals. Even though Neanderthals were smart tool makers, they were stronger. However, Cro-Magnon had superior intellect. They were better tool makers. They created better hunting strategies. Against animals and probably the Neanderthal. In disputed territories, Cro-Magnon would almost always win. And they did win. We are proof of that."

Kelly turned to Grenier, "They could never leave and they could never give birth?"

Grenier nodded. "Remember, all the Gemps are Government property."

The silence hung between the three.

"We'd have to euthanize them." Steve said.

Kelly interjected, "How horrible!"

Grenier shrugged, "Probably not kill them. This group is doing a very good job of that. The population is down by a third in the last several months. This group cannot reproduce. It will die out."

Steve asked, "Why?"

"They've broken up into different groups. Two of the groups seem to have declared war amongst each other. Attacks are regular and vicious."

"My God!" Steve exclaimed.

Grenier stated, "This would have happened with or without you. I'm just glad you are overseeing the controlled group."

Steve shook his head, "But what will happen to Mos' group?"

Grenier let a slight smile slip out for a second. "We have data from the last couple years like you wouldn't believe. Not just from a sociological standpoint." He left it at that.

"Ken, what are you not telling us?"

Grenier let the smile return. "Classified."

"Don't pull that shit on us now. You've spilled . . ."

"I know, too much now. Just believe me when I say the Gemps below are a dead end evolution wise."

Chapter 5

It was 1:39 am and Kelly couldn't sleep. Neither Steve nor Kelly felt like talking when they got back to their room. They checked in on Oscar, who was fast asleep and dreaming. Both washed up, ate a quick meal from the pantry and went to bed. Then, she just woke up. "Steve, you awake?"

Steve snoozed softly while drooling on his pillow.

"Steve! You awake?"

Steve rolled over. "Not yet. Why?"

"Because I can't sleep."

With his back still facing Kelly he said, "And you want me to share in your insomnia?"

"No, well . . . no . . . yes. I do."

Steve yawned and rolled back over.

"What are we going to do about the Gemps?"

"Which ones?"

"Both."

Steve took a deep breath. This was going to be a long night. "Kelly. Government property, remember? I don't like it either, but we both signed the dotted line. Uncle

Sam is paying for our retirement."

"But they are alive. They think for God's sake. They think and have emotions."

"I know, but I don't think Ken meant Mos' group would be killed."

"That's not how I heard him."

"Ken said the wild Gemps are an evolutionary dead-end. He said no such thing about Mos'."

"Steve, that's the point. One group gets killed . . ."

"Maybe. We don't know the big picture."

"Okay, one group may get killed and the other something. What's the something? Research? Medical experiments. Zoos?"

Steve thought a moment. 'Zoos.' Very illogical, but who blames the Government for thinking logically? "I think there really is something bigger going on here, but I'm too sleepy to talk about it. Just a few more hours . . . of . . ." and he started snoozing again.

Kelly watched him. "Should she be mad? She gave the thought a few minutes to germinate. Yes, she should be. He fell asleep while they were talking. She thought she should give him the silent treatment in the morning and have him wonder what he did wrong all day. Men! Never quite understanding what is important.

***

Steve woke up with a start. He dreamt he was talking to Kelly in the middle of the night and fell asleep while they were talking. He shook the fogginess from his head. It was just a dream he eventually convinced himself. Steve stretched, yawned, and got up. It was 5:30 am. The morning briefing would be in another four hours, so he decided a quick wash up and a trip to the base gym, before breakfast, would be a good thing. When he got there Kelly was already working a Stairmaster. He walked up to an empty station next to Kelly. He climbed up and leaned in to say 'morning'.

Kelly saw when Steve walked in. He spotted her, smiled, and stopped at a station next to her's. She pretended not to notice him. When he leaned in to say 'hi' she looked away casually.

Steve tapped Kelly on the shoulder.

She turned, said, "Morning," then looked away again.

Realization hit Steve. It wasn't a dream. He'd known Kelly long enough to know that she'd find an in to tell him what he did wrong. He sighed deeply, placed the earplugs attached to his smartphone into his ears and started exercising.

***

Oscar had left that morning early. He had an agenda. His destination would be the Gemps. It was worked out. He'd seen it on Television many times. He watched some of the male soldiers use it on the female soldiers and civilians. PFC Haynes greeted him at one of the secured entrance into the Gemp camp. This entrance was made especially for him.

"Greetings Oscar," the young private said.

Oscar gave him a toothy smile.

Haynes checked today's activity. "Oscar, I don't see an authorized schedule outing today."

Oscar signed, "Special assignment. Very important."

The young man eyed Oscar, "Is that so? Is this something I can mention to Dr. Launse when I see him?"

Oscar hooted a few times. He worked his mouth as if he were talking to Haynes. Then he produced an L-Ration card. Steve had about three years' worth stockpiled in his office. It was meant to be used on the mainland.

Haynes smiled. The last L-Ration card Oscar gave him had about three hundred dollars on it. The card disappeared somewhere in the Private's pants pocket. He simply said, "I'll let Reynolds know you are out. Treat him well, too."

Oscar raised the fingertips of an open right hand to his lips and he gently moved them away as if blowing a kiss. In a way, it was just that. This was more than a thank you if it worked.

The path to the village was long. It usually took about 30 minutes if he wasn't in a hurry. When he emerged from the hidden passageway the Sun had just started to rise. It was another fifteen minutes' walk to the village. Oscar had decided he would approach Hela, first. Whenever he was in the village she seemed to pay more attention to him. She was also the most attentive student he had whenever he taught them new signs. As a backup plan, he brought chocolate. He quickened his pace and made it to the village fringe in less than five minutes. He slowly approached Hela's shelter. Stepping around to the entrance he quickly peered inside. Empty.

She had to be down by the river.

He causally walked the short distance and found her with Feme. Both had found fruit and were washing it for an early meal.

Feme heard the break of twigs first. She turned thinking it would be Tutu and one of the other Gemps. She tapped Hela when she saw the Elder. Both giggled as the Elder slowly made his way toward them.

Oscar signed, "Children. Morning. Good to see pretty Hela and Feme."

Both signed and said, "Elder. We are surprised to see you."

Oscar replied, "Really? God sent me to check on his children."

Hela and Feme excitedly ran up to Oscar.

Feme signed, "Elder, it was frightening last night. The sky flashed bright many times followed by loud boom sounds."

Hela followed with, "And Mos ran into the village. He said God made the light and sound."

Oscar signed, "And Tutu did not believe him."

"Elder!" Hela said. "How did you know?"

"God sent me to check on his children."

The two Gemps were excited. They giggled. "Elder, you must tell the village."

Oscar signed, "Stop. Not yet. Elder wants to talk to both of you."

The two settled down. "Yes, Elder?" Feme said.

"The Elder favors you two."

They blushed.

"You have a special place in Elder's heart."

They giggled and leaned into one another.

"Elder would like to show how much he favors Hela and Feme. Will you let me show you?"

Hela asked, "How, Elder?"

"May I touch you in a special place?"

They blinked.

"Come. Let's not wake the others yet. Let us go into Hela's shelter. Just the three of us."

They hesitated. "Are you going to hurt us like Tutu and Gitu?"

Oscar shook his head. "Elder favors the two and will be kind. He has a treat." Two pieces of chocolate appeared in his hand. He finger spelt, "C H O C O L A T E." He motioned for them to eat it.

Each Gemp took a piece. They sniffed and lightly licked at the heart shaped milk chocolate pieces. Each piece was as big as a thumb.

Hela pronounced, "Choke O Late?"

Oscar bit into air and signed, "Bite. Surprise inside."

Feme bit first. Her eyes widened and she savored the sweet innards. She sucked in the gooey cherry gel leaving the heart empty.

Hela watched Feme. It must be good she thought

and took a bite. The cherry flavor mixed in with the milk chocolate coating burst into her mouth. She look at Oscar, who was staring intently at her, and wanted another. The deliciously gooey filling coated her teeth and tongue and made her salivate.

Both signed, "More, please. May I have another?"

Oscar smiled, "Elder wants to favor Feme and Hela. We go to Hela shelter. Oscar has appetite for pretty Feme and Hela."

The two blushed and still licking their lips walked, without a word back into the village. Everyone was still asleep, which was good. They walked passed Kiri's shelter and heard what sounded like Mos' voice. They knew what he was doing. He favored Kiri. Now Elder was going to favor them and both became excited. The Elder was going to give them more chocolate. As they reached Hela's Shelter, both Gemps looked at each other and nodded. Elder knew God and he had chocolate, too.

***

Steve set his tray of fruit, toast, and Greek yogurt next to Kelly.

She was eating a bagel. A half empty cup of coffee was in her hands. She stared blankly at a wall behind

Steve.

"Kelly, I'm sorry. I was so tired, I . . ."

". . . asleep while we were talking."

"It was one something in the morning."

"1:39 am . . . and you fell asleep. This was important."

Steve knew it was fruitless to argue. He would never win this battle. It wasn't worth the mental ammo. "Kelly, I am sorry. Really. I'm awake now."

"The moment passed," She said.

Steve sighed.

The two ate in silence.

A few minutes later Grenier walked into the cafeteria, spotted Steve and Kelly. He hurried over to the two with an alarmed look on his face.

Kelly noticed Grenier first. She reached over and touched Steve on the sleeve, her anger forgotten. "Steve," she said.

Grenier sat down. "Steve, we have a situation."

"The Gemps?!?"

"Worse, Oscar."

Kelly said, "Oh my God. Is he okay?"

"You two need to see this." He got up and left.

Kelly got up first with Steve very close.

All three walked into Briefing Room Three. It was

the only room with a large 110 inch flat screen. Rogers, the morning shift supervisor, sat at one end of the conference table. He had a media control tablet in front of him. Colonel Codper, scowling, sat at the other.

Kelly and Steve sat in the middle on one side, Grenier the other.

Kelly, still worried, said, "Is Oscar alright?"

Codper spoke, "More than alright, Ma'am. Damn near perfect."

She gave him an inquisitive look.

Grenier nodded at Rogers.

Rogers tapped on the tablet a few times. The lights dimmed and the flat screen came on. He moved out of the way so that the others could see the entire screen. "At 0545 PFC Haynes allowed Oscar unauthorized entry into Gemp Village One." He narrated.

The screen showed several images of Oscar moving through the passageway. The first few moments he was moving at a regular pace, then suddenly he picked up his pace and practically started running. Clearly he was on a mission and agenda of his own making.

Rogers tapped at the tablet.

The video changed to Oscar with Hela and Feme by the riverbank.

Codper asked, "What is he doing?"

Steve watched with dread. He followed the conversation. "Oscar is tempting the two."

"Tempting," Codper began, "Tempting them for . . ." his voice trailed off.

Everyone watched as the camera showed Hela and Feme each eat a heart shaped chocolate filled with something. Kelly identified with their reactions. Then the three headed into the village. The video switched to show the three entering Hela's shelter. The screen went dark.

The room remained silent for a moment.

Codper said, "Did that little chimp of yours do what I think he did? Did he fornicate with the Gemps?"

Steve turned to face the Colonel. "I can't believe Oscar would . . . shit."

Codper said, "Son, that little bastard monkey of yours is out of control."

"I take offense to that, Colonel. Oscar is not out of control and he is not a bastard."

Codper stood up, outraged, yelled while pointing to the screen, "What did we just watch?"

"Oscar doing what . . ."

Codper yelled, ". . . he's not supposed to be doing that."

"Colonel, he's still an animal with urges. He's . . ."

". . . fucking those beast!"

Kelly had a distressed look on her face. She thought for a moment and said, "Isn't this exactly what we wanted?"

Everyone tuned to face her.

Grenier said, "Kelly, what do you mean?"

"Think about it. Oscar is the only one on this base who either doesn't have a partner or can't go to the mainland for outlet. He's stuck on this island with humans and Gemps."

Steve sucked in his lips, "She's right. I hadn't thought about that. Damn!"

Codper said, "So we let this chimp of yours fornicate with the Gemps?"

Grenier said, "Yes."

Codper turned, "What?!?"

Grenier turned to Steve. "Steve, what have men in power done over the ages?"

"Most have abused it. History is full of examples."

Grenier said, "What about religion?"

Steve said, "Some of the worse examples of abuse."

Codper sat down, "Outrageous. No man of God would ever abuse his position."

Steve replied, "Colonel, the bible is full of examples. Maybe it's how you look at it?"

"There is only one way to read the Bible, son. It is . . ."

"Haman."

"Pardon?"

"Haman, Colonel. He was the vizier of King Ahasuerus. If it wasn't for Esther the entire Hebrew nation would have been wiped out. And there's Herod. Judas. Pilate. Simon. All men of power. The bible shows that eventually those who abuse power fail and fall."

Codper nodded. He had just finished reading Matthew 26 and 27. "Okay, son. I get it, but that still doesn't excuse the fact of your little monkey fornicating."

Grenier said, "Colonel, you're missing the point. This is a fluid experiment. Nothing is set in stone here."

The Colonel was about to call Grenier son but remembered last night. "What do you suggest we do?"

"Steve, I think this is the best thing to happen. Think of it. Oscar is showing us the development of corruption of power. He's learned to work the system and is now using it to his advantage. We got two experiments going here."

Steve took a deep breath. Grenier was right. He looked over to Kelly.

She smiled. Even though it was gross on some levels she also saw it as very sweet. Oscar having a girlfriend or two.

"Okay, we let Oscar continue, but I think we should punish him in some way."

Codper said, "I'm not likely this one bit. This project seems to me is getting out of hand."

"In what way?" Grenier said.

Codper remained silent. Civilians he thought. Non believing heathens.

"Colonel, we are gathering information."

"At the tax payers' expense." Codper spat.

Grenier retorted, "And the Military cost what each year?"

Codper stood up.

Grenier stood up and leaned forward. "The project is not in jeopardy, Colonel."

The two men stared at one another for an undetermined amount of seconds.

Codper blinked again. "A standing army is vital in a world full of evil."

Grenier answered, "Especially when we are the cause of such evil. Colonel, look, we walked into this project knowing that all sorts of unknowns were going to pop up. This is one. It won't be the last."

Codper sat down. "I'm adding this to my report to the Chairman."

Grenier nodded, "And I'm adding this to my report to the President and Joint Chief of Staff."

Steve and Kelly held their breath. Codper and Grenier clashed before, but not like this.

Rogers coughed. "Sirs, briefing is in another 30 minutes."

Codper said, "Understood."

Grenier looked at his watch. "My suggestion is to not mention this incident while Oscar is here. I'd like him to think he got away with his adventure."

Codper said, "And that will accomplish what?"

"Let him continue. We can observe him and the Gemps. That is the reason we made him 'The Elder'."

Steve nodded, "True, but for him to think he got away is . . ."

". . . is good. Let's work this out. How far will he go? Will the other male Gemps challenge him? Will God's might be enough for Oscar to keep his position? We just had another can of worms opened. Plump and juicy. I say we let it ride."

Kelly nodded. "I agree, but for different reasons."

All the males turned to her.

Grenier asked, "Such?"

"It's not that I like the idea of Oscar turning into an alpha dominating misogynistic male, but that Hela and

Feme are in a position of power. You've read the book, 'The Power of the Pussy', right?"

She got blank stirs.

Men she thought. Bright as door knobs sometimes. "Look, Oscar wants something. Apparently, he went to great lengths to get it. I used to think men had it so easy in enticing women, but I'm seeing it differently now. First, Oscar had to be in a position that got him noticed. Next, he had to dream up his plan. He needed the means and materials. Then he had to execute it. If anything, I'd wonder how one, Oscar got the chocolate and second, got PFC Hayes to allow him to leave unauthorized. Guys, Oscar has been working the system for years to his advantage. Seems to me, we wanted to make Gemps human. Instead, we made a chimpanzee human as well. But anyway, as I was saying, Hela and Feme are in a position to work the system themselves. They are getting chocolate in exchange for Oscar's needs."

"Fornicating!" Codper spat.

Kelly continued, "The Gemps have been sexually active for about a year now and . . ."

Codper said, "Disgusting little beasts."

Kelly scowled, "Disgusting? Colonel, are you living in the Dark Ages?"

"I just don't like the thought of all this."

Kelly eyed him for a few seconds, but decided to not push. Clearly the Colonel had issues but this was not the time to air his dirty laundry. She said, "Oscar should continue and, of course, we should watch him."

Grenier nodded, "Colonel, I know there has been a breach in discipline and protocol in one or more instance, but I strongly urge you to allow it to continue. Talk to PFC Hayes, if you must, but don't spook him. Punish him later, but not now."

"Don't tell me how to discipline my men . . ."

Grenier raised his voice a little louder than he had wanted, "God damn it Colonel! No one is stepping on your dick . . ." He blushed, turned to Kelly, "Sorry," turned back to Codper, "This is an opportunity of getting good data. This, as odd as it seems, is the reason for spending all this money. The emergence of Human behavior, good, bad, or indifferent, by non-humans." He was red in the cheeks. If he could have the Colonel replaced he would, but the Chairman favored him. Fuck! Grenier thought.

Codper stared at Grenier a long time. He'd let the little monkey continue. He'll have the duty sergeant watch Haynes closer. He'll give Garner what he wanted, but he would recommend to the Chairman the project be terminated, and the Gemps destroyed. He'd see

Grenier pushing the unemployment line and it would be good. "Alright. We'll let the little chimp continue . . . for now."

"Thank you," Grenier said.

***

Oscar used up his quota of chocolate for the month early. He had another week of waiting and that was much too long. Feme and Hela wanted chocolate and he wanted them.

Sergeant Farmers was behind his desk. He knew Oscar wanted something the moment the little chimp rounded the corner. "Oscar!" He signed, "Hello."

Oscar jumped up onto a chair next to Farmers' desk. He signed, "Chocolate. You have?"

Farmers said, "Of course, Oscar." He smiled. "I always reserve extra for you, but . . ."

Oscar produced a L-Ration card.

Farmers leaned back into his chair. "How many boxes?"

Oscar remembered the first time he tried this. He asked for one box. When he came back for another Farmers said he needed another L-Ration card. Oscar was so furious he thought about ripping the man's arm off and beating him with it. He learned over the years. He signed, "Give me two now. Two next week. Two week after that."

Farmers nodded. The chimp learned some bargaining over the years. Besides, he liked Oscar. Everyone did. Oscar had a cache of L-Rations and that made it even better. "Done. Flavor filling, nuts, or solid?"

"One box flavor. One box mixed, please."

A few minutes later Oscar had his two boxes. He hurried to his room to drop the boxes off before this morning's briefing. He'd ration them out to Feme and Hela over a week time. Today he'd get his outing schedule.

Chapter 6

After the morning briefing Codper went to his room. "Heathens!" He spat. The bottle of whiskey sat next to his computer keyboard on his desk. He reached for the cup next to it and blew inside. He poured a healthy dose of booze and swallowed half of it in one gulp. Then filled the cup again and sipped this time. He sat back in his chair and stared at a blank monitor. His bible was within reach and when he touched it he immediately felt at ease in a way adult beverage would never make him feel. He turned to Deuteronomy.

"Neither shalt thou bring an abomination into thine house, lest thou be a cursed thing like it: but thou shalt utterly detest it, and thou shalt utterly abhor it; for it is a cursed thing." – Deuteronomy 7:26

He finished the cup and poured another.

***

Oscar had a feeling that something changed. Everyone in the room avoided looking at him directly. It took him years to understand that when humans look you in the eye it is not a challenge. He sat in between Kelly and Steve. Kelly smiled down at him and gave him a hug. She almost never did that. Steve made idle talk. He asked about his evening and did he read anything special. He asked if he wanted to talk about something. Oscar caught a frown from Grenier. It disappeared when he saw Oscar staring and he smiled. The Colonel was in a foul mood. He was almost always in a foul mode. Recently, he started smelling like naughty-water. This morning was no exception. His face was scrunched up during the entire meeting, but that meant little to Oscar. He was thinking of Hela and Feme and this morning. He started to become excited again, but quickly thought of something else. Like TV and video games, but both the Gemps sure felt good. Everyone agreed he should visit the Village daily, which of course he didn't mind. That was the best news. Ever.

***

"But when the righteous turneth away from his righteousness, and committeth iniquity, and doeth according

to all the abominations that the wicked man doeth, shall he live? All his righteousness that he hath done shall not be mentioned: in his trespass that he hath trespassed, and in his sin that he hath sinned, in them shall he die." – Ezekiel 18:24

He poured another.

***

Oscar hurried to his room. He found a small pouch he could use to carry some chocolate. He put in some chewy filling ones and a few with nut centers. He hoped the first box would last a couple of days.

***

"Watch and pray, that ye enter not into temptation: the spirit indeed is willing, but the flesh is weak." – Matthew 26:41

He poured another.

***

Oscar emerged from the passageway and casually

walked to the village. He made his way to the river bank and entered from there. Most of the Gemps were sitting around grooming one another. Hela and Feme sat near Mos and Kiri, talking. Mos had picked figs earlier and now shared them. Kiri had several pomegranates between her legs. She handed one to Mos and another to Hela and Feme. They looked up and saw Oscar.

***

"There hath no temptation taken you but such as is common to man: but God is faithful, who will not suffer you to be tempted above that ye are able; but will with the temptation also make a way to escape, that ye may be able to bear it." – Corinthians 10:13

His hand slipped and some whiskey missed the cup.

***

Steve, Kelly, and Grenier sat in the observation room. Two of the large monitors were focused on Mos and those around him. Oscar came into view and sat in the center. Hela and Feme blushed and acted shy. Mos signed, "Elder, Mos has questions about God."

Oscar replied, "My child, ask."

Grenier leaned back in his chair, "If only I had popcorn."

Steve shot Grenier a quick glance, "Ken, this is serious. What are we doing?"

Grenier leaned forward to get a better look at Steve, "We just doubled down. All that happens now is just profit. Nothing lost everything gained." He leaned back again.

Kelly asked, "How so?"

Grenier answered, "Oscar. Ironically, he's our human link.

***

"I will make mine arrows drunk with blood, and my sword shall devour flesh; and that with the blood of the slain and of the captives, from the beginning of revenges upon the enemy." – Deuteronomy 32:42

He misjudged the distance and grabbed air. The second attempt he grabbed cup and drank.

***

Oscar signed, "God is like us, but taller. He is smart. Knows a lot about many things. He watches us. He takes care of us." Then Oscar remembered the key item he had to slip in. He took his right index finger, lifted up his left elbow to his chest level and struck it lightly and quick with the index finger. He finger spelled "PUNISH".

The three imitated Oscar.

Mos pronounced it, "Poo-nish."

Oscar shook his head and signed "Sounds like RUN." He hooked a right hand index finger "L" around his left hand index "L" thumb. Both hands had the index fingers parallel to the ground with the thumbs up. He quickly thrusted both hands away from him quickly.

Mos nodded, said,"Pun-ish."

Oscar gave him a toothy smile.

The others pronounced the word.

Oscar clapped.

Feme asked, "What does this word mean?"

***

"And after all that is come upon us for our evil deeds, and for our great trespass, seeing that thou our God hast punished us less than our iniquities deserve, and hast given

us such deliverance as this; Should we again break thy commandments, and join in affinity with the people of these abominations? wouldest not thou be angry with us till thou hadst consumed us, so that there should be no remnant nor escaping?" – Ezra 9:13 - 14

He stopped drinking. He was satisfied with his heavy buzz.

***

Oscar signed, "God would take away all that is good. No food. No shelter. No clothing." He looked at Hela and Feme. "No chocolate."

Mos and Kiri gave Oscar a curious look.

Hela and Feme frowned and tears welled up in their eyes.

Oscar continued, "Listen to God. Follow his ways and his teachings through me and you shall be rewarded."

Mos said, "I believe in God." He pointed to himself, pointed to his forehead and clasped his hands together in front of him. He finger spelt "IN" and finished with a right hand index finger to the sky and bringing the hand down open palm fingers slightly spread palm facing left to chest level.

***

"For the stars of heaven and the constellations thereof shall not give their light: the sun shall be darkened in his going forth, and the moon shall not cause her light to shine.

And I will punish the world for their evil, and the wicked for their iniquity; and I will cause the arrogancy of the proud to cease, and will lay low the haughtiness of the terrible.

I will make a man more precious than fine gold; even a man than the golden wedge of Ophir." – Isaiah 13:10-12

He turned on his computer and waited precious seconds for the welcome screen to appear. His email program started immediately. Within a minute he saw a message from the Chairman embedded in a stream of other messages. He clicked on the Chairman's and read. It was a simple email. It read,

My good Colonel,

I agree, the situation is dire and deserves further congressional oversight. The President, the Joint Chief of Staff, DARPA and the NBAC are behind this project - fully. This is not a battle that can be fought by

committee.

"Then I proclaimed a fast there, at the river of Ahava, that we might afflict ourselves before our God, to seek of him a right way for us, and for our little ones, and for all our substance.

For I was ashamed to require of the king a band of soldiers and horsemen to help us against the enemy in the way: because we had spoken unto the king, saying, The hand of our God is upon all them for good that seek him; but his power and his wrath is against all them that forsake him.

So we fasted and besought our God for this: and he was intreated of us." – Ezra 8:21-23

May you find the strength, my friend, to do what is right in your heart.

With all sincerity,

B.

His heavy buzz faded quickly. He was on his own now. A pity.

***

Tutu walked over to Oscar. He said and signed, "Tutu, not believe. No proof."

Oscar stood up. He was still a foot shorter than Tutu, "Do I look like Tutu?"

Tutu frowned, said, "No."

"Do I talk like Tutu?"

"Elder has no voice. Talks with hands."

"Proof God exists. I am different, yet we talk. We . . . "

"Do not see the same thing. I see small Gemp. Hairy. No voice. God is flawed to make Elder funny looking."

Oscar's anger flared up. He thought about hitting Tutu, but decided Steve would be mad and take away his chocolate and TV. He did once before. Oscar screamed and broke anything and everything that was throwable, but Steve stood there and waited. When Oscar finished Steve flew into a chimp-like crazed rage. He chased Oscar around the room screaming, yelling, and throwing things at Oscar. The chimp was terrified. That was the last time Steve had to react extreme. Oscar looked Tutu in the eyes. Steve told him to make sure he doesn't blink first.

Tutu stared back. No one challenged him before like this. The Elder locked gaze and never let up. Tutu felt a growing coldness creep up his back. He was losing his nerve. The Elder won.

Oscar watched as Tutu looked down.

Tutu, feeling disgusted, said, "Tutu no like God or Elder." He looked at Hela and Feme. "Follow me."

Both said, "No."

Tutu gave them a scowl.

Both females stood up and signed, "No."

Tutu, forgetting his encounter with Oscar roared.

The other Gemps around the village scampered from the center. Tutu was mad and someone was going to get hurt.

***

An alarm went off in the Command center. Steve, Kelly, and Grenier were still in the observation room talking. Grenier clicked an intercom button near his seat. "This is Grenier, who triggered that alarm?"

A specialist stood up, 'Sir! Gemps are about to fight."

One of the large monitors showed Tutu puffing out his chest, roaring.

Grenier turned to Steve, said, "Might be a good time to show God? I'm worried that Tutu might hurt Oscar."

"Oh, Steve, Oscar could get hurt." Kelly said.

Steve shook his head, "It's the other way 'round. Oscar is strong enough to rip Tutu to pieces. The Gemps only have two-thirds our strength."

Grenier pressed the Intercom button. "Prepare Mr. Launse for a Day launch. Start to que up clouds and place a rain storm on stand-by." He turned to Steve and released the button. "Agreed?"

Steve nodded, "Agreed."

Grenier pressed the button again, "Mr. Launse is going out in five minutes. Prepare a subterranean launch."

Steve took a deep breath and exhaled. "Kelly, ready? This is it."

She nodded and the two raced out.

Grenier sat back down and wished he had that bag of popcorn. He pulled out his cell phone and called the kitchen. Cookie was on duty. "Cookie, can you bring up a large bag of your home style popcorn to Observation Room one, please?"

A deep voice answered, "Of course, sir. Up in five minutes."

"Perfect! Thanks, I owe you."

Cookie answered, "Tens and twenties, sir."

Both men laughed before Grenier clicked off.

***

The Colonel woke with a start. The alarm sounded. He had been hunched in his chair, in front of the computer. He reached for the phone and dialed the Command center. "What's the alarm about?"

The voice replied, "Gemps, sir. Possible fight. Mr. Launse is about to go out."

Codper grunted, "On the way." He slammed the phone down, contemplated taking another drink but in mid pour changed his mind. He walked into the bathroom and rinsed his mouth in hot water and mouthwash. Damn apes he thought. Abominations, the whole lot.

***

Oscar stepped in front of Tutu. "Both said no," he signed. He knew Steve well enough to know that fighting to protect the Gemps would be okay.

Tutu roared. He swung at Oscar.

Oscar ducked and was glad to have an excuse to hit Tutu. He gave him a two arm slam combo.

Tutu felt Oscar's powerful hands connect. He would not have thought the small chimp could hit so hard. He swung at Oscar again.

Oscar ducked and hit him with another two arm combination. He yelled and hit a third time.

Tutu fell to the ground. He pushed himself away from Oscar and ran to his shelter. He emerged with a bow and arrow.

Oscar stood his ground and snarled.

Tutu took aim.

Hela stepped in front of Oscar and stare hard at Tutu.

Tutu looked up and said, "Hela move. I shoot Elder, not you."

Hela slowly shook her head. "No."

Tutu aimed again.

Feme stepped in front of Hela.

Tutu looked up, growled, "Move, Feme!"

"No." Feme said.

"Then I shoot you first."

Mos and Kiri stepped in front of Feme.

Tutu yelled, "Move! I shoot everyone!"

No one moved.

Tutu roared and ran at the group.

Oscar launched himself at Tutu, chimp screaming the short distance. He avoided Tutu's grab and bit him on the arm. Oscar screamed and started beating Tutu with outstretched arms.

Tutu fell to the ground, curled up into a ball, taking the crazed chimp's powerful arm blows.

Suddenly the ground shook. Fruit from nearby trees dropped to the ground.

Mos fell to the ground, "It is God! God must be angry."

Oscar stopped hitting Tutu. He ran and hide behind Feme and Hela signing, "God mad God mad God mad."

Tutu tried to stand up. He grabbed at the nearest shelter and pulled himself up. Oscar didn't break anything, but he would be feeling the small creature's attack for days. It would be a painful reminder to never piss off a chimp.

Steve heard Oscar's shrill scream over the intercom. Kelly had just finished putting on the last touch of makeup. She rigged him a harness that had a capacitor at the small of his back. It stored enough electricity to drop a raging bull elephant at 20 yards away. With a flick of his wrist, stream of bolt, elephant down. He turned to Staff Sergeant Erwin, who operated the ground shaker and tunnel lift to the surface.

Erwin flipped the switch and massive metal pads underneath the village started vibrating. Randomly a pad would recoil away from the surface and strike hard.

Erwin said, "Ready, sir?"

Steve nodded. He was standing in a bowl like platform.

Erwin flipped another switch and two halves of an acrylic cone sealed together to protect him from dirt. Erwin flipped a third switch and Steve started to rise. The surface above him opened up and dirt poured in around him. The platform caught most of it. Fog rolled in and covered the gaping hole Steve was emerging from. Once out in the open the two acrylic halves separated. Dirt spilled in and covered his feet.

The ground stopped shaking and smoke appeared out of nowhere. The bright sky started to turn dark and a hole appeared in the ground. Kiri grabbed Mos' hand and squeezed tightly. All the Gemps watched as a hooded figure appeared from the ground. Mos recognized the figure. He said, "It is God."

Steve stepped away from the platform and walked over to Mos.

Mos dropped to his knees and said, "God, I knew you would be here."

Steve looked down, "Mos, my emissary, no need to kneel. Stand."

Tutu walked over to Steve and stared intensely. The hood hid most of Steve's face and Tutu squirted. He strained to see detail but only saw shadowed outlines. "Tutu not believe in God. Hate Elder and you."

Steve grabbed Tutu, "Do not fight The Elder!" He gave Tutu a quick shock. "Ever!" He tossed him aside.

Tutu, terrified, shook. He blinked several times and remained on the ground.

Steve said, "I am here to guide you, but if you disobey and resist I can punish." He made a gesture for Erwin to amp up his volume for a few seconds on the hidden embedded speakers around the village. "Follow me and I reward. Disobey me or the Elder I will punish!" The threat reverberated throughout the village. The shelters vibrated, as designed, to echo Steve's words.

He walked over to Oscar. Lifted him up to his face and whispered, "Love Oscar. Follow. Treat later." Then said loudly, "Do not fight my Gemps! They are to be loved and cared for." He tossed Oscar aside. "Return home, Elder!"

Oscar, torn with feelings, ran off into the jungle. He made his way to his secret entry way. He heard Steve say 'Love Oscar. Follow. Treat later.' But was scared at what he saw. On some levels he comprehended what Steve was doing. On other levels he was still a chimp that feared the unknown. Technology was magic and powerful.

***

Grenier was half-way through his bowl of popcorn when the Colonel walked in. Grenier caught a whiff of whiskey seconds before the Colonel entered the observation room. It wasn't strong, but it was noticeable enough to know the Colonel liked his breakfast grains liquid.

Codper looked at Grenier and the bowl of popcorn. He frowned at the man.

Grenier looked up and smiled. "Sorry, Colonel. You'll have to get your own bowl."

"No doubt," Codper said. He hardly contained the look of disgust.

"You missed the beginning, but it looks like this might be a good movie."

Codper stared at the screen. "I'm not liking this."

Grenier took a deep breath. "Okay, what is it you're not liking?"

"This whole farce."

"Colonel. Why are you here then?"

Codper wanted to deck Grenier.

"You knew from the beginning what this program was about. You knew what Steve would be doing. You watched this operation from day one and . . ."

"Hadn't thought it through. I didn't think this project would have gone this far."

"And now that you see it?" Grenier put the bowl of popcorn aside.

Codper didn't say anything.

"Colonel, this is going to be a problem." Grenier got up and walked out.

Chapter 7

Codper made it to his room late. He had lunch, alone, in the cafeteria. Abominations! He thought. He canceled his meeting with the Duty Officers – there was nothing he wanted to talk about anyway. Captain Pierce had requested morning prayer sessions, but Codper hadn't committed. A conflict of interest lingered in the back of his mind. He sighed and scanned his desk. The bible was nearby, next to the keyboard. He walked over to his desk and sat. He reached over and grabbed the book, the comfort he needed. A random page:

"And I said unto them, Whosoever hath any gold, let them break it off. So they gave it me: then I cast it into the fire, and there came out this calf.

And when Moses saw that the people were naked; (for Aaron had made them naked unto their shame among their enemies:)

Then Moses stood in the gate of the camp, and said, Who is on the Lord's side? let him come unto me. And all the sons of Levi gathered themselves together unto him." – Exodus 32:24-26

His other comfort lay within a foot. It was a third full. His cup had dust in it. It always did when empty for more than an hour. He blew into it and wiped the lip clean. Some of the whiskey splashed droplets on his desk as he poured. Those he let dry. The one's that landed on his bible he wiped off. He randomly picked another page and read:

"Draw out also the spear, and stop the way against them that persecute me: say unto my soul, I am thy salvation.

Let them be confounded and put to shame that seek after my soul: let them be turned back and brought to confusion that devise my hurt.

Let them be as chaff before the wind: and let the angel of the Lord chase them." – Psalm 35:3-5

He said aloud, "God! Please give me a sign. I am torn over this. I want to do right but I need your guidance." He clicked on the email program on his computer and finished the cup. He poured another cup while a stream of subject lines scrolled down the screen. The stream stopped and one email caught his eyes. The title was, "New Assignment Orders. Read Immediately." That he opened. It was directly from the Joint Chief and it was brief. His official orders were on the way, but effective immediately he was fired. End of message. He nearly dropped his cup. After staring at the email for nearly five minutes he drained his cup, got up and walked out of his room.

***

Grenier was at his desk when he heard the new email indicator. It was from the Joint Chief. The first half of the email was what he expected. Codper was being replaced, immediately. The official orders were forthcoming. The second half of the email took him by surprise. He exclaimed, "Fuck!" The Colonel got his wish after all. "Bastard!" The ending confused him. He was to continue as Director of a new phase in the program. Steve, Kelly, and Oscar were to stay as consultants. His new orders would be sent in by carrier within the new few days. Odd. He got up and walked toward the door. This was something he had to talk to Steve about. Interesting he thought then he realized what the new phase would be. By the time he reached the door he was giddy. This was going to be a great day. As he started walking out he nearly bumped into Codper. Before he could say something Codper recoiled an arm and struck quickly. His fist connected with Grenier chin, launching him backwards into his desk. Grenier rubbed the hit off and braced himself for another attack.

Codper stepped past the room threshold. "You fuck! You had me replaced! I ought to kick your ass! You ruined my career!"

"You're the one who went Dark Age on me. You had one job to do and that came into question. What do you expect?"

"You blind-sided . . ."

"As if you hadn't tried to blind side me? The Chairman left you to hang, friend. You got eaten by your own kind."

"Non-sense!"

"You better fuck non-sense, because no one else will touch you."

Codper rushed in with an uppercut that felt air.

Grenier sidestepped and slammed an open palm into the Colonel's temple. He didn't want to kill the man, so he scaled the blow down.

Codper's head hit the edge of the desk. He collapsed

and stayed down.

Grenier said, "You fuck! How dare you come into my office like this. You medieval son-of-a-bitch. Take your bible thumping ass and leave!"

Codper slowly got up. He realized Grenier had better skills. "This is not over," he hissed as he gave himself some distance from Grenier.

"The hell it better be over. Fuck with me and you could kiss your pension goodbye."

"Don't threaten me!"

"I just did. Now get the fuck out or I'll have you carried out breathing or otherwise. Your choice."

Codper eyed the younger man intensely. He had better skill that was certain. "This is not finished."

"Colonel, don't write checks with your mouth that your ass can't cash."

Codper backed out of the room, "Fuck you!"

"And that god damn stupid horse you rode in on." Grenier spat.

Seconds later all was quiet. Codper gone, Grenier sat in his chair. He'd give Steve and Kelly the news later. The silly pompous pious ass Grenier thought. One job and he couldn't do that right. He took several deep breaths to relax. After punching in the base intercom code on his phone he announced, "Attention all personnel. Attention all personnel. Colonel Codper has been relieved of duty by the Joint Chief of Staff. Under no circumstances are you obligated to follow his orders. His replacement is enroute. Until then, Captain Pierce is temporarily in charge." That should take care of most of the personnel he thought. It was the small faction of devotees that worried him. It was no secret the Colonel held bible studies on Sundays. It was also no secret that most of the attendees leaned just as far right if not further. Grenier sucked in his lips as he realized Captain Pierce leaned just as hard to the right. "Fuck!" was all he could say. He quickly tapped out a message to the Joint Chief.

"Request immediate military personnel replacement. Predict conditions will devolve to dangerous levels."

Message sent.

***

Captain Pierce knocked on the Colonel's door.

Codper had just finished nursing his fourth cup of whiskey when he heard the knock. He was not in the mood to have guests. He took another sip. "What?!?"

The Captain's voice from behind the door said, "Colonel, we need to talk."

"It's unlocked." Another sip.

Pierce walked in. "This is not right, sir."

Codper nodded and pursed his lips. "Yeah. Short of shooting the fuck I can't do anything."

Pierce eyed the older officer. He sucked air through his front teeth making a sharp smack sound. "Why don't you, sir?"

Codper looked up from his cup. "My pension. That's why I won't."

Pierce stepped in closer. "Sir, the little prick is playing with fire. Government project or not. It's not right. We know how you feel about those things. Most of us agree."

Codper stared the younger man in the eye. "It's your problem now."

Pierce nodded. "Not what I wanted to hear."

Codper drained his cup. The whiskey still stung on the way down. He hadn't drank enough to take care of that.

"Son, I've been doing this far too long. I'm tired. The world is fucked and you want me to kill my enemy?"

Pierce nodded, "Sounds about right."

Codper poured himself another. "What would you

have me do? Take over the base. Murder everyone and blame those abominations?"

"It's still sounding right to me, sir."

Codper eyed the man.

"We could release the other Gemps, let them run wild in here. Afterward we burn this place to the ground. Grenade those with bullet wound to the head to remove traces."

"Thou shall not kill."

"Bullshit, Colonel! We are soldiers. That's what we do. These are our enemies. They are creating creatures outside of God's realm. You've been outspoken for weeks now. This is the time to do something."

Codper started to pour himself another drink when suddenly Pierce stopped him.

The young man held a vise grip on the bottle.

"Let go." Codper said.

"Sir, you in or out?"

"Let go."

Pierce released the bottle.

"I'm in. But we have to remove all traces."

Pierce smiled.

Chapter 8

Steve, Kelly, and Oscar were still in the lunch room when Grenier approached their table.

Kelly gestured for him to join.

Oscar jumped from his seat.

Grenier caught him and gave Oscar a head bump.

The chimp grinned teeth and cooed.

Grenier sat down placing Oscar next to him. "I got good news and bad news."

Steve nodded, "We heard the announcement over the PA."

Grenier smiled, "That's part of the good news."

Kelly asked, "What's the bad news?" She had her hand on Steve's arm.

His smile faded, "Because of our friend the Colonel, the project is being shut down."

"That's terrible news!" Steve said.

Kelly asked, "What's going to happen to the Gemps?"

Grenier's smile returned. "We're moving to phase 2 of the project. We are . . ."

Steve said, "Wait. Phase 2?"

Grenier nodded. "You didn't think Uncle Sam would use the Gemps for religious studies their entire lives?"

Steve slowly shook his head.

"At some point we'd have to deal with superstitious Gemps. Now is probably better than later."

Steve took a deep breath, "Okay, what is phase 2?"

Grenier stood up. "Follow me to my office and we can talk."

***

Pierce and a dozen soldiers stood in the Colonel's room.

Codper had put the bottle down and now faced them. He shaved and had his ACU on. The bible was in his left hand. "Those creatures out there are a threat to the natural order of things. In our arrogance we created life in His image, but life as an abomination. An unpure monstrosity that mocks our very existence. This mockery ends today."

The men around him nodded.

Pierce stepped out. "Colonel, of course, we're with you. They have to go. Everything has to go."

Codper asked, "I take it you've worked out details?"

Pierce rapidly sucked in air between his front teeth. The smack sound was loud. "Of course, sir. And with your approval."

Codper studied the young man. Was he one to trust? Probably not, but how was he supposed to save his kind. "Let's hear it."

"First, we gather everyone into one room. Then we capture some wild Gemps and toss them in the room with the others. We shoot a few folks and Gemps and toss in some grenades. Then we release the other Gemps and hunt them down under the pretense they are dangerous. Once that's done, we call in for help. Blame everything on the Gemps and a few soldiers not with us. While we were out getting the village Gemps, the "other" soldiers got too sloppy. We can guess the wild Gemps either got the grenades by accident and not knowing what to do killed themselves and everyone in the room or some fool soldier held on too long. We stick to our story that we tried to round up the village Gemps and the deed is done."

Codper nodded. He liked the plan. Factor in the fog of war and Pierce had a pretty good plan. "And we are the survivors."

Pierce nodded. "We give each man in this room a story to tell. Not the same story of course, different enough. Someone was by the door. Another person was down the hall. Someone saw some Gemps in the building. Some did not but heard Gemp screams."

Codper nodded.

"We'll also have to beat ourselves up a bit to make it convincing we fought for our lives. But we can pull this off."

Codper slowly smiled. "We could pull this off. I like it."

"Thank you, sir." He turned to face one of those is the room. "Donalds. Turn off the video and audio feeds. Internal and external. McKinney, you, Rich, and Smithie release the wild Gemps. Capture a few and cuff'em. Ford, Luke, Rogers, Threatt, secure the control room. The rest is with me and the Colonel. We'll round up Launse, Grenier and the others. I got more of us guarding the exits just waiting for the word."

Codper thought a moment, then quickly nodded. "Let's do this."

***

Grenier walked in first and sat behind his desk. Steve and Kelly took a seat with Oscar jumping into Steve's lap.

"Would anyone care for coffee?" Grenier asked.

Oscar signed, "Coffee, please."

Grenier smiled. "Certainly, Oscar. The usual amount of sugar and cream?"

Oscar signed, "Yes, please. Sugar, yum."

Grenier got up and walked over to a small kitchenette at the corner of his office. "First, phase 2 is about teaching the Gemps basic common core lessons." He put in two scoops of instant coffee grounds into a coffee mug. Oscar's name was stenciled across the side. "The government wants the Gemps taught at a college level and . . ."

Steve interrupted, ". . . taught! As in attending school?"

Grenier scooped in two heaping piles of sugar using a small spoon. He poured about two seconds worth of cream. He stirred the spoon as he poured hot water into the cup. After a moment of stirring he walked over to Oscar and handed the cup of coffee to him.

Oscar took the cup and sipped. Just the way he liked it.

Steve cleared his throat, "As in attending school?"

Grenier nodded slowly, "Something like that."

Kelly leaned forward, "Ken, what are you not telling us?"

No need to withhold any information now, Grenier thought. "Space is a pretty dangerous place . . ." He continued before Steve or Kelly interrupted, ". . . so is underwater exploration. So is sub-terrain discovery expeditions. Sending Soldiers behind enemy lines is also dangerous work." He paused for several seconds. "You see where I'm going with this?"

Steve horrified, answered, "I do and I don't know how I'm feeling about that."

Grenier turned to Kelly. "What are your thoughts?"

Kelly looked at Steve and Oscar, then back at him. "It'll initially save their lives?"

Grenier thought she had been the quicker of the two. Steve was much too nostalgic and emotional. Kelly he liked a bit more than he often admitted. She was more pragmatic.

"What about their rights?" Kelly asked.

"As of now, they have none. They are all property of the United States Government, but to put your mind at ease, they will not be overlooked per se."

Steve interjected, "Per se?"

"The Gemps are highly intelligent creatures. They have emotions. They think and more importantly, they can learn, of which is what makes them valuable."

"They shouldn't be thought of as property." Steve

said.

Grenier shrugged and held it for a few seconds. He pursed his lips and raised but eyebrows. "I don't have an answer for that. Not a good one. But I can tell you, that one day the Gemps will be granted full US Citizen status. But not today. Maybe not in a few years."

Steve asked, "How come?"

"We had a hard time dealing with a debt ceiling. We have ultra conservatives in our government who'll toss out the baby with the bathwater. We've been working quietly to get this far. The Gemps are under a provision that guarantees humane treatment and plans for their free retirement."

Steve shook his head. "So much I'm not quite getting."

Oscar kissed him on the cheek.

Grenier continued, "The Gemps will be allowed certain privileges . . ."

Kelly asked, ". . . like?"

"Clothes, foods, certain types of property, some things we have to educate the population first before they can walk freely. We're working out the details of pay . . ."

Steve frowned. "Pay?"

"Yeah. Even if the Gemps aren't citizens they will

still work. We can't call them beast of burden. They aren't farm animals. The one advantage they have, unlike the dolphins or Oscar, is that they can articulate emotions, desires, wants, and needs. Can you imagine the lawsuits from ever Lib-organization on Earth if we didn't treat them like people?"

Steve's frown deepened.

"Steve, this nation still can't quite get it right with minorities. How do you think the neo-conservative is going to react to genetically-engineered super-intelligent teenage-like chimps walking freely? We'll have another sort of problems with the active left as well."

Steve started, "But . . ."

Grenier said, ". . . no buts. Warm and fuzzy this can't be yet."

Steve took a deep breath. "Okay, what is our role?"

Grenier relaxed a bit. "Mentor and instructor. I'll be getting involved in this phase."

"As what?" Steve asked.

Oscar finished his coffee and stretched out on Steve's lap. Coffee made him feel good but sleepy sometimes. Or it could have been that he was only able to understand and follow a small part of what Grenier talked about. Humans talked too much sometimes.

They made him sleepy.

"Depends on the task."

Kelly added, "Mission?"

Grenier nodded. "Yeah, the mission. I just don't push paper."

Suddenly the alarm went off.

Grenier punched in the speed dial code to the Main Command center. It rang a dozen times before he got a disconnect tone. "Fuck! This is not good." He walked over to the door and opened it. Just as he suspected. "Greetings Colonel, Captain Pierce, I was just . . ."

Codper punched him in the face a second time today.

Grenier stepped back a few feet and rubbed his jaw. "That hurt."

Codper drew his pistol and pointed it directly at his face. "You pompous ass. Give me a reason not to shoo t you in the face now." He stepped up close to Grenier. Pierce and the rest had M16-A2s pointed at him.

Grenier grabbed the gun and pressed it hard against Codper's thigh dislocating the trigger finger at the knuckle.

Codper bit down a yell.

Grenier pulled the gun away and pointed it at Codper's face. "You pompous arrogant ass back. Any other time I would have shot you in the face and not given you a second thought. I know how this is going to play out." He pressed the magazine release and caught it with his left hand. Bullets flipped toward Codper's face as he emptied the magazine. He tossed the magazine across the room and dismantled the Beretta M9. He chucked the barrel behind his desk and spun the handle at Codper.

Codper was nursing his dislocated finger when the handle clipped him across the forehead. It left a nasty gash. The Colonel took a deep breath and popped his finger back in place. He walked over and gave Grenier a slap with the other hand. "You . . . you . . ."

Grenier walked out into the hallway. Other soldiers stood attentive with pointed M16s.

Oscar signed, "Me bite Colonel?"

Steve signed back, "No bite Colonel. Bite will make you sick."

Codper faced Steve and Kelly. "Launse, Ma'am, please follow Grenier."

Oscar growled.

Steve grabbed Oscar's face, "No growl. Be good." He and Kelly walked into the hall way and followed Grenier and the other soldiers.

Codper said, "Nasty beast. If I had my gun I'd shoot the thing."

Pierce watched everything. He liked Oscar. Pretty much everyone did. Strike three for the Colonel.

***

Grenier heard several explosives. His first impulse was to run toward the sound. The M16s at his back squelched it. A second impulse wanted him to take Steve and the others in the opposite direction. The smell of death was in the air and he saw no happy ending to this day.

Codper moved ahead and hurried down the stairs. The doors to one of the rooms had been blown out. Scorched body parts and debris littered the entrance. "What the fuck happened?"

A nearby soldier said, "Someone tried to be a hero, sir. Boom."

Codper turned to face Pierce.

Pierce shrugged. "There's more than one room. You want to shoot them in the back?"

Codper answered, "I wanted this to be clean and quick. Now it's . . ."

Grenier never let him finish. He grabbed the nearest M16, switched the selector to single shoot and squeezed the trigger once at the soldier's face. Blood splattered in all direction. He squeezed off several more shots – all hitting dead center. "Run!" He yelled.

Steve and Kelly ducked behind a station desk. Bullets sprayed the area in fits and blurps across the room.

Grenier squeezed off several single shots in seemingly random directions – all finding a target.

Then, the shooting stopped.

Grenier looked up and saw several Grenades tossed his way. Five second fuses he thought as he jumped over the desk and caught two mid-flight. He twisted and threw both at the emergency door across the room. He landed near Steve, Kelly, and Oscar. One second to go he thought as he dragged the desk just enough to shelter everyone from the blasts.

Oscar screamed as the first grenade blew. He squeezed Steve's neck tightly. The blast pushed them and the desk several feet. Two more explosions went off further away.

Grenier's ears rang. He shook his head to clear the fog.

Steve, Kelly, and Oscar seemed alright. Steve looked as if he were about to pass out. Oscar had a death grip, with long chimp arms, around his neck.

Grenier grabbed everyone and made them run to the

new hole in the wall. The emergency doors gone.

Codper waited several seconds after the grenades went off. He stepped in the room and expected to see body parts and blood splatter everywhere. "What the fuck!" Only desk and computer debris scattered the room. He looked around and saw the emergency doors missing. Things got complicated.

***

Tutu sat against a large rock near the remains of an old fire. Burnt logs buried in ashes jetted out. Tonight they would start another fire and roast corn from the mystery box. He finished one apple and started eating a second one when he smelled dirty fur. He wrinkled his nose and turned to the forest edge. Immediately, the hair at the back of his neck stiffened. Intruder.

"Food," the figure said.

Tutu strained to see the figure just inside the tree line. It hugged close to the ground.

"Food. Food want."

Tutu took several steps back adding some distance between him and the strange creature. "Show self. Then food get."

The figure retreated further into the forest

Tutu took a step forward, stopped, thought a moment, took several more steps back. "Want food. Show self."

The figure moved. It was quick.

Tutu tried to track it visually as it faded further into the forest. Moments later the figure was gone and he heard a scream. He turned and ran. It was from one of the female village Gemps.

Strange looking Gemps had invaded his village. Within seconds the village was overrun by filthy intruders. A wild Gemp jumped him. He twisted underneath it and swung his arm backward. He felt his fist contact teeth and something gave way. The wild Gemp lay motionless on the ground. A wild Gemp was on Mos trying to bite his neck. Tutu clenched his hands together and gave it a powerful downward blow to the head. The wild Gemp's skull caved in and the creature went limp.

Mos looked up and gave Tutu a "thank you" sign.

Both Gemps looked on and attacked as many wild Gemps as possible. Two jumped on Mos. Three on Tutu.

Oscar ran ahead of the others. He heard the commotion and feared the worst. Hela and Feme in trouble. Hurry he thought. Hurry. Hela Feme in trouble. Must help. Run faster. On some subsurface level Oscar knew things had suddenly changed. The Colonel, Pierce, most of the men on the base. They were different. The explosions. The pieces of people and the shooting. All scary. All terrifying.

Lulos was on the ground. She struggled as a wild Gemp tried to mount her. She screamed, kicked, and screamed more.

The wild Gemp became rock solid. This he was going to enjoy. He grabbed Lulos' neck and started to squeeze. Just as he was about to enter Oscar jumped him. Powerful chimp arms pounded hard about his head and shoulders. The wild Gemp tried to get away, but Oscar's attack was relentless. Moments later the wild Gemp stopped fighting back.

Steve, Kelly, and Grenier arrived to see Oscar step off the dead Gemp. They heard several screams toward the center of the village.

Oscar moved first. These were his Gemps. No creature he thought would harm them. Ever. The wild Gemps were attacking the others. Grenier ran over to two wild Gemps attacking Mos. Both were biting at and hitting him. Grenier grabbed one Gemp and placed a choke hold on it. It screamed and clawed at his face. Seconds later it went limp. A second later Grenier broke its neck. He hated to, Uncle Sam's money or not, this was survival now.

Mos swung upward and hit the other Gemp in the jaw. It broke but the thing continued attacking. Mos swung again as hard as he could. His arms ached. He swung again and again. He hit the face. He hit the head. He hit the head again. And again. And again. He stood over a dead Gemp.

Steve stood motionless watching pandemonium. He saw Grenier and Oscar in action, helping as they could. Even Kelly tried to help. She kicked at a wild Gemp trying to rape a female. She pulled its hair and punched its face. Soon, both females were beating the poor creature into unconsciousness. Then a wild Gemp jumped on Kelly. It bite her in the shoulder and she screamed. He acted. He screamed like Oscar and struck at the animal. His anger was primal and fierce. His attack was ruthless. The wild Gemp cringed as Steve pounded with all his might. Kelly was his love and no man or creature would harm her. He continued pounding at its chest and skull until it lay still. He breathed hard, his heart pounding. Murder is what he just committed. With his hands. He turned on the other wild Gemps. A dozen left. Attacking. He leapt into action alongside Oscar and fought. Both of them crazed creatures raining powerful blows down on the invaders.

Mos looked on in awe. God and the Elder defending the village. The screams the two made. High pitched and terrifying. Mos looked at both his hands and made fists. He joined the fray, not quite getting the yell right. But after a moment he too was caught up in the frenzy. Arms high, power down, scream loud. Make the wild ones fear their wrath. The wrath of God, Elder . . . and the Messenger.

Then . . . silence.

The village littered with dead and wounded wild Gemps.

Steve was bruised badly across the cheek and arm. His clothing torn.

Kelly's face was covered with dirt, her makeup smudged.

Oscar's robe colored with dirt and blood.

Grenier looked perfect. His suit wrinkle free and his hair neatly combed.

Mos walked up to Steve, "God, you saved us."

Tutu walked up to Steve. He looked at Grenier and

Kelly, then turned his gaze back to Steve. "Something not right. There is more than one of you. And these other Gemps?"

Grenier and Kelly walked up next to Steve. He faced Tutu. "You are right." He looked at Mos. "We have to talk. Things are about to change. And I have to be honest with you."

Mos said, "Honest? With me?

Steve nodded. He looked at Tutu. "Others like us may be coming. The others are bad. They are the reason these other Gemps are here."

Tutu growled. "Hate other Gemps. Crazy." He then looked at Steve, Kelly, and Grenier. Clothing strange, faces strange, all things strange. "What does God mean?"

Steve answered, "You have to send the village Gemps in the forest. To hide. I fear the worst."

Tutu repeated, "What does God mean?"

Grenier leaned close to Steve. "I think he wants to know the meaning of God. Not what you are saying as God."

Steve looked at Grenier for a moment, then he looked at Tutu. Those eyes Steve thought. Tutu is the one, not Mos. "Tutu, I am not God."

Mos, distressed, said, "God must not say such things.

Mos see great scary things from God."

Steve knelt down. "I wish we had time to explain, but we really must hide. Everyone."

Grenier said, "I called in a support team earlier. Don't know how long they will take so, in the meantime, keeping out of sight is best."

Tutu said, "We will stay. No run."

Steve frowned. "Tutu, we are not running. We are hiding. We . . ."

". . . no, I am not God. We . . ."

". . . must hide." Steve stressed.

Tutu shook his head slowly. "No."

Steve looked to Grenier.

Grenier said, "We're probably priority one. The Gemps are secondary. "

Oscar suddenly looked alert. He pried into the forest toward the main building. He growled.

Grenier said, "Yeah, I don't like them either. We should leave now. Staying in the village is definitely not in the Gemps best interest."

Oscar yelped and jumped into Steve's arm.

Grenier lead the way. He and the others disappeared in the forest.

Moments later Tutu heard a rumbling sound.

Mos stepped up next to him. He strained his eyes. "I hear sound too. Things are different now."

Tutu nodded.

The rest of the village Gemps started to assemble near Tutu and Mos.

Kiri stood next to Mos.

Hela and Feme were near.

The sound got louder and the ground vibrated.

Tutu caught a whiff of exhaust. He wrinkled his noise and growled.

A moment later a Humvee crashed through the tree line, followed by several more. Most of the Gemps scattered. Mos thought they looked like wide hollowed out tree trunks. Men like 'I am not God' came through wearing strange colored clothing. They had thick sticks and strange tree branches in their arms. One of the strangers held a small "L" shaped stick. He pointed it at one of the Gemps. Thunder and smoked ripped from a hole at one end.

Mos watched as blood spattered from the Gemp's head. It crumpled to the ground. Fear gripped Mos. God had been right. "Run!" He yelled out, "Run!" Tutu ran with him as rapid thunder erupted from the thick sticks and branches the evil creatures held. "Run!" Kiri, Hela and Feme were near and followed as Mos crashed through the jungle. The last time he ran he met God. This time it was because of God again.

Codper saw the vile creatures scatter into the jungle. He put a bullet in one of them and it felt satisfying. "Kill them all!" He shouted. "Kill them all!"

Chapter 9

Captain Pierce looked on as his men and the Colonel hunted the Gemps down. He thought they would have made great pets – especially the females. He watched the bootlegged copies of more than one Gemp sex video. Some of the soldiers, he thought, were sick perverts. They talked about how big the Males got and called them Nickers. When he finally caved in and watched his first video he came within minutes. His guilty thoughts on how young the females looked made him sick to his stomach. It took five more viewings before guilt disappeared entirely. Now he was shooting them. He gave a heavy sign as one female came into view. She was running toward him not looking. He lifted up his rifle and laid the crosshair square center of her chest. She had small breasts that jiggled tightly as she bound over rocks and fallen tree branches. He pulled his finger away from the trigger and quickly scanned the area near her. She was alone. Pierce's palms started to sweat. He moved the scope back on the Gemp. She was still running toward him. He shouldered his rifle and slid behind a tree, waiting. His strike would be swift.

Wela ran as fast as she could. The bad creatures had been hurting the others and she had to find safe shelter.

Pierce waited and heard the Gemp rapidly move his way. When he saw an outstretched furry arm he grabbed it.

Wela was too shocked to say anything. The bad creature's grip was powerful. He pulled her in close to his chest and put a hand around her mouth. She found his thumb just above her lip. His other hand started groping her chests. She tried to scream but his hand gripped tighter around her mouth. She grabbed his wrist and pulled down. His thumb touched her lips and she clamped on to it with her teeth. He hit her in the back of the head. She bite down hard between the distal joint. Skin gave way and her teeth cut neatly through muscle, tendon, and cartilage. He pushed her away screaming at her. She backed off and spat the thumb out of her mouth. He aimed the rifle and squeezed off a round. The bullet missed her heart but pierced her left shoulder slicing through the lung and shattering the top part of shoulder blade. She fainted.

Pierce cursed himself and spat at the Gemp. He stepped up to Wela and rolled her over. He ripped her loin-cloth off making her cheeks quiver. He stared at her butt and fantasized abusing it until the arch in his thumb became unbearable. He wrapped the cloth tightly around his wound and considered his options. "Stupid little bitch." He uttered. "I ought to fucking rape your chimp ass." He stared intently at Wela licking his lips. He sucked in air between his front teeth and lips. The pain in his thumb faded. He knelt down on top of Wela and started rubbing himself on her. He could feel himself aroused and he rubbed harder. He pulled himself out and started stroking with his right hand. "You vile little bitch. I'm gonna make you suck." He rolled the unconscious Wela on to her back and moved himself up to her mouth. He played himself across her lips getting himself wet. When he was about to explode he slipped himself into Wela's mouth and pumped fervently. Seconds later he erupted. His entire body spasmed like never before. It was intense and extreme.

Wela woke up with a start. The bad creature had himself in her mouth and she nearly gagged when he jismed. She was not afraid this time, but angry. No male Gemp would do such a thing unless given permission.

She looked up and saw the bad creature, with closed eyes, shaking. She scowled and bit down as if she were biting into a rock. Stiffened tissue split and her upper and bottom teeth met hard. The man screamed loudly as blood pumped out from what was left of his penis. Wela had bitten off more than half. The bad creature fumbled for his rifle. Wela coughed strongly causing her to gag and vomit the soft piece out. She hissed at Pierce, wiped her mouth and disappeared into the forest.

Pierce fired his rifle at the receding Wela. His aim was off due to throbbing pain from two embarrassing wounds, which could never be adequately explained.

***

Grenier made it to a crop of rocks at the bottom of the mountain. Kelly and Steve, breathing hard, emerged from the jungle tree line and collapsed at Grenier's feet. Oscar had been sitting on a ledge, waiting, for some minutes. He knew the area well.

Grenier said, "Okay, we make a stand here . . ."

Steve, still breathing hard, said, ". . . what stand? They have guns we have nothing."

Grenier shook his head, "Wrong thinking. We have

everything we need. We have Oscar, you, Kelly, myself. We have rocks and the high ground . . ."

Steve said, ". . . we can't fight guns with rocks!"

"We have to hold them off until the cavalry arrives. Might be hours, might be days. But we have to try. Hiding is not an option. Not with me."

Steve answered, "Fuck!"

Grenier squared-off in front of the younger man, "Steve, trust me on this. We have the advantage."

"I want too, but . . ."

"Steve, why this spot? I ran you guys three miles through dense jungle to here. Oscar knows this place, you should too."

Steve, breathe caught, looked around. He spotted a remote camera high in one of the trees. Near the base on the mountain he spotted a strange pattern of rocks. They were stacked rather neatly. The bottom rock had a small black ring near its bottom. The top rock had a small metal nipple in front.

Grenier interrupted his thoughts, "You remember now?"

Steve smiled. Hope was not lost.

Tutu caught the Elder's scent quickly. I am not God's scent was faint but distinct. He wanted answers.

The village was attacked by dirty smelling Gemps and bad creatures. He quickened his pace.

Mos followed Tutu through the underbrush. This area on The Place was thick with trees and plants. Further out was the salty water and the sand. There were lots of scary caves that held strange lights and sounds. Mos had forgotten about the caves. He remembered an encounter some time ago and started to slow down.

Kiri came up beside him, "Mos, you slow down?"

Mos picked up his pace. "Mos okay."

Kiri wondered.

Grenier entered the access code to the observation room. It was situated deep in one of the many caves that dotted the mountain side. The last time they used it was about two years ago, but it was still functional and had a cache of food, clothing, weapons, and communication equipment.

Tutu followed the scents to a cave entrance some ten feet above the ground. He remembered this one in particular. Strange noises and lights came from deep inside it. At the time he was afraid to further investigate. He was young and scared easily back then.

Mos remembered this cave as well. Tutu told him of

the lights and noise. He was curious and made the long trip to see for himself. Smoke was coming from one of the rocks and he heard moans. The fur on the back of his neck stiffened and he couldn't go any further. Now he stood in front on the very cave that scared him not so long ago.

Kiri, Hela, and Feme stood next to the two male Gemps. They noticed the expressions on each of their faces. Tutu was purposeful. Mos was dread.

Grenier had just settled into a command station. He flipped the power switch to the chamber earlier and waited a minute for all the computers and systems to come online. A proximity alert went off. "Fuck! Not now!" He typed in a code and the remote cameras searched the area. Tutu, Mos, and several other Gemps were at the base of the cave. He smiled and exhaled. Maybe this was the best time to wean the Gemps off mother's milk. "Steve," he said, "we have company."

Steve stepped over to the Monitor. "We have to get them in here."

Grenier nodded, but for different reasons. "I'm changing the access codes to all the doors . . . belay that. I'm leaving the exterior door alone. We'll have to pull out some food before the Colonel and friends finds us."

Tutu and Mos helped the other Gemps scale the ten foot climb to the cave entrance. Mos caught the Elder's scent. He wasn't sure if he should be glad or upset.

Tutu stepped into the cave first.

Mos hesitated a moment.

Kiri placed a hand on his shoulder, "Mos . . ."

Mos nearly jumped. He gave Kiri a glance and he followed Tutu into the cave.

Steve stepped out into the tunnel and stayed within the shadows. He watched the Gemps inch their way along the cave wall until Tutu was about five feet in front of him. "Stop." He said.

Tutu, startled, hissed. He squinted his eyes and a faint image of Steve appeared. "What are you?" Tutu asked.

Steve stepped into the dimmed light of the cave. "Human. My real name is Steve."

Mos asked, "Not God?"

Steve said, "Mos, I am sorry. I deceived you. I am called a human. The bad men who invaded your village are also humans."

Tutu asked, "Why?"

"Why the bad humans?"

"Why?" He repeated.

"Follow me and we can talk."

"No." Tutu said.

Steve knelt down. "Tutu, the bad humans are still out there looking for us. We are not safe in the tunnel. Follow me into safe shelter and you'll start getting answers."

Tutu hesitated.

Mos said, "I will follow, Go . . . Steve."

Steve stared into the Gemp's eyes. He recognized the look of disappointment, or it could have been a projection of his own feelings of guilt and disappointment. He stood up and walked to the hidden door entrance. Mos, Kiri, Hela, and Feme stood behind him. It took Tutu a few seconds to make up his mind. He followed Steve.

Chapter 10

Codper stood in the middle of the Village. The ground was littered with dead Gemps. A deep satisfaction can over him as he stepped over several little bodies. To his right he heard a female Gemp scream. Then a single shot. Two soldiers walked out from the forest laughing. One of them said "HumanTD", both laughed again. Codper lifted the walkie-talkie to his mouth. "Captain Pierce, report."

Nothing.

"Report!" He clicked the Talk-Button twice. "Has anyone seen the Captain?"

"Sir?"

Codper turned away. "Yes?"

A sergeant stood with his M16 pointed down at the ground. "You ought to see this."

"Lead the way, son."

***

Steve walked through the disguised door. Oscar

spotted Hela and Feme and ran to them. They embraced one another.

Oscar signed, "Glad you are safe and here."

Hela said and signed, "Elder, explain what has happened."

Grenier stepped into the light. He waited for Tutu, Mos, and Kiri to enter. The heavy door clicked shut. "I can explain."

All the Gemps turned to Grenier.

"Strange, I know. But if you can give me a few moments you will have some answers. Follow me." Grenier lead them into an adjacent room.

***

The Sergeant took Codper through a path of broken low hanging tree branches. Even before the Colonel reached the spot he smelled death. "Damn!" He said as he saw Captain Pierce sitting up against a tree. His rifle's barrel rested against his right thigh, the rest of the gun between his legs.

Codper knelt down and noticed the wound in his chest. Must have had it on auto when it went off he thought. Then he looked down and saw Pierce's blood soaked crotch. "What happened?" Codper asked, but he felt he knew. Suicide?

"Not sure, sir. One of the Gemps, maybe?" The Sergeant had a sense of what happened, too.

Both men looked at each other. Codper blushed deep red, the Sergeant a shade lighter.

"Sir?"

Codper stood up. "Is the Lieutenant nearby?"

"He was chasing down some Gemps last report over the radio."

"Find him. We need to get Grenier and the others to pull this off. Start checking the outposts."

The sergeant saluted, turned, and walked away.

***

Grenier sat in one of the chairs. "Please have a sit."

The Gemps looked at one another.

Grenier said, "It hasn't been that long since you sat in a chair."

They hesitated.

Oscar pulled out a chair for Hela and Feme. He sat in a chair next to the two.

Hela sat first, then Feme, both looking like small adults in a large playroom for giants.

Tutu sat next. He jumped over the armrest and

planted his bottom solidly on the chair seat.

Mos lifted himself up cautiously. He had a look on his face as if he remembered something. He looked over to Kiri, who was seated next to him. She nodded and recognized his expression. She, too, remembered something familiar about a table and chair.

Grenier cleared his throat. "Thank you. My name is Grenier. First, I have to apologize. You may not remember this, but not too long ago you sat in chairs like these. You sat at a table and listened to a human, standing in front of the room like this one, teach you how to talk. A human taught you how to eat, cook, make bows and arrows. A human taught you how to . . . "

Tutu yelled, "Enough!"

Grenier sat quietly, but he did not avoid eye contact with Tutu.

After a moment Tutu looked away, "I not believe you."

Grenier nodded. "Fair enough. I'll be right back." He walked out of the room for a moment. He returned with a remote control in his hand. "I'd like to show you something then."

Tutu watched the human as he moved his thumb across a small black strip of wood. A large white cloth came down from the top of the ceiling. "What is this?"

He hissed.

Grenier ignored him for the moment. He thought, 'this is theater, my suspicious friend' and smiled.

Tutu looked across the room at the others. He was uncertain as how to act. Should he just attack the humans? Or wait. Then he remembered how Elder and Not God now Steve fought off the dirty Gemps. The screams they made. The death they created. He would wait.

Grenier press his thumb on the small bit of wood. The lights dimmed and a projector dropped from the ceiling. "What you are about to see is moving mind images projected onto this white cloth. It's not magic. It is called technology. So, please do not be afraid." He pressed the play button.

A large human face appeared on the screen. Feme jumped and screamed. Oscar jumped over to her chair. He hugged and cooed. Tutu and Hela hissed at the face. Only Mos and Kiri remained silent.

Kiri frowned. She remembered something about the face. It was comforting and caring and happy.

Mos looked over to Kiri. He frowned, too. "Mary?"

Kiri turned her head to face Mos. She nodded.

Grenier said, "Mary Austin is her name. She was one

of many caregivers who worked the farm."

Tutu walked over to the screen and peeked behind it.

Grenier paused the video. He would wait.

Mos and the others walked over to Tutu.

"No one is here?" Tutu said.

"It is a projection. An image of the person. Like looking into the lake except we can show the image many times, anytime."

"No one is here?" Tutu repeated.

Mos said, "No one is here."

Hela said, "No one is here."

Feme said, "No one is here."

Kiri said, "No one is here."

The Gemps circled the projector screen several times crossing in front of the light.

Grenier waited patiently. He liked what he saw.

Steve watched with fascination as the Gemps inspected the screen. A few moments later Tutu grabbed a chair and started scrutinizing the projector. He found the keypad controls and pressed a red button. The projector powered off.

Oscar bantered and moved over to Steve.

Steve smoothed Oscar's hair as the little chimp's teeth clicked.

Grenier pressed the on button.

Tutu and the other Gemps jumped. Tutu pressed the red button again. The projector blinked out.

Grenier pressed the on switch.

Tutu pressed the red button.

Lights on, lights off, lights on, lights off, light on.

Mos said, "Tutu. Grenier turns thing ..."

"Projector." Grenier interrupted.

". . . projector by small piece of wood he is holding."

Tutu walked over to Grenier.

Grenier moved the control away as Tutu tried to snatch it from his hand.

Tutu hissed.

Grenier, taking his cue from Steve, hissed back and louder.

Tutu hadn't expected that. He remembered Grenier dishing out his own brand of death on the wild Gemps. He backed down.

Grenier said, "Ask me nicely and I'll give it to you."

Tutu stared.

Grenier stared back.

Tutu blinked first, "I changed my mind."

"All right by me, but I would like you to sit back down in the chair so that I may continue."

Tutu stood his ground.

"You wanted answer, yes?" Grenier said.

Tutu nodded.

"Then please sit back down."

The Gemp stood fast.

"Please, Tutu. Answers. Promise."

Tutu frowned and walked back to his chair. He sat in a huff. The others were already seated. The large human face was still on the screen. "Mary."

Grenier continued, "She was one of your caregivers." He resumed the video.

Mary said, "Hi!" She stepped back to show a thin blonde hair young woman with a bright smile. Her hair was tied back with a pink bow. She wore bright pink spandex pants and a green cotton top that was partly covered by a long white lab coat. When she talked she seemed to bubble and gush. "Welcome to the Farm. My name is Mary and I'll be your host." She giggled.

The Camera followed Mary throughout the tour. It stopped and focused on a group of very young looking Gemps. Tutu was standing over a young Mos and Kiri.

Young Tutu was angry and yelling at the two, "My toy! My toy! My toy!"

Mary ran over and rubbed Tutu's chest. "Yes Tutu, your toy, but you can share. It will always be your toy until you decide to give it away. But, right now you are sharing."

"My toy!"

She smoothed his head and said, "Strong Tutu, your toy."

"My toy!"

Mary changed her voice, "Tutu!"

He was startled and looked her in the eyes, "Brave, strong, wise Gemps share. Your toy, but you like to share."

He nodded and relaxed. "Tutu will share."

The scene changed. Hela and Feme were playing with blocks of wood. Oscar walked over, sat next to the two. Kissed each one on the cheek, knocked the blocks over and ran. Feme and Hela chased Oscar, knocking things over, laughing and screaming. Steve appeared.

"Oscar!"

Oscar playfully screamed while being chased. He ran into Steve knocking him down. Hela and Feme stepped on Steve as they followed.

The scene changed again. A room filled with Gemps seated behind desks were listening to Kelly recite the alphabet.

Another change. Grenier is staring into the camera. He is holding it. "Hopefully we're onto two stage by the time you see this. I am sorry. But if you are seeing this video I apologize again. You don't-didn't believe me. You don't-didn't remember who I am. You don't remember Steve, Kelly, or when you first met Oscar. Making you forget was necessary. Now it is necessary you believe and we move on. Enjoy your new freedom. This is where life will get exciting and you have a purpose. Learn everything . . ." A young Tutu snatches the camera. "Learn learn learn learn learn." Grenier gets control of the camera again. He's relaxed and smiling. "Until then."

A collage of different scenes played on the screen. A few minutes later the video ended.

Grenier turned on the light.

Mos stared at Steve. "I don't remember, not God anymore but now is Steve."

Steve nodded, "You will, in time, but now you'll have a whole new world of learning ahead of you. You'll see things as I and Oscar Elder sees them. You'll . . ."

"I am mad." Tutu said.

Grenier nodded. "I know."

"I am mad at you and the other humans."

Grenier nodded again. "I understand. But I need your help now."

"No help."

"I will help." Mos spoke up.

Kiri added, "Mos help, I help."

Feme and Hela nodded.

Tutu asked, "Why would I help?"

"Brave, strong, wise Gemps help. That's why."

Tutu's face relaxed after a second. He nodded. "Tutu will help."

Grenier smiled. Damn that conditioning was strong.

Chapter 11

Codper had a large map of the Island spread across the hood of a Humvee. A dozen locations were circled in an odd misshapen circle.

A walkie-talkie chirped several times.

Codper grabbed it, "Alpha-base, ready."

The voice crackled several times, "Outpost four and five are negative. Moving to post seven. Post one and twelve last. Over."

Codper X'ed out the circles marked four and five on the map. Seven, one, and twelve were left.

***

Grenier held up a handgun that was converted to shooting tranquilizer darts. "This is called a magazine and it holds six darts." He pulled a bullet out from the magazine. "This thin covering breaks away the moment the bullet leaves the barrel." He pointed to the front end on the gun. "You squeeze the trigger toward you to fire the gun. The gun will kick a little, so you have to hold it firmly in your hand." He placed the magazine into the pistol grip. Slide back on the barrel and let it slide forward. He took the gun off safety, aimed at the far wall of the storage room and squeezed the trigger.

Tutu and the others jumped from the gun's bark.

"Outside the gun won't sound as loud." He walked over to a black chest marked 'weapon accessories' and opened it. He pulled out plastic eye protectors and headphones for the Gemps. The humans got earplugs.

Steve and Kelly helped Oscar and the Gemps with their headphones.

"Tutu, you first. I want to show you how to fire this gun."

Tutu slowly walked over. He understood that squeezing the trigger made it bark, but he was still apprehensive enough to eye it cautiously.

Grenier positioned Tutu with the gun in his hands.

"Tutu, place your index finger here along the barrel." He tapped Tutu's index finger. "Get a firm grip. It will jump out of your hands if you hold it too lightly." He made sure Tutu had a firm grip. "Place the tip of your index finger on the trigger." He had to push the finger tip over the trigger. "Pull the tip of your index finger toward . . ."

BANG!!!

Tutu nearly dropped the gun.

"Very good. Do it again."

Bang!!!

Tutu did not jump as dramatic as before.

"Better. Fire again."

Bang.

Grenier nodded. "Fire again, but this time on your own."

Tutu did and he liked it.

Grenier went through the steps with the other Gemps.

Feme dropped the weapon once.

Mos dropped it three times.

Kiri and Hela fired the weapon like pros.

Grenier, satisfied the Gemps could fire the weapon without killing themselves, moved to the next stage. Teaching them how to aim and to safely carry the gun. Reloading was last.

One hour later Grenier decided it was time to break. All his Gemps learned at a phenomenal rate. They all had excellent eyesight and aimed with deadly accuracy.

"Time to eat." Grenier said. He walked over to a storage box marked MREs. Pulled a dozen out and handed a pack to each person. He ripped the top off with his teeth and spilled the contents onto the conference table. The Gemps mimicked him.

Steve opened Oscar's.

Fast learners Grenier told himself. Very fast. Almost too fast. As everyone ate he got up and walked over to the weapon's accessory box. He pulled out communication earpieces. He tapped on a small button on the side of each comm-piece. Only one needed a new battery. He walked over to the table and handed everyone an earpiece, including Oscar. "Tapped this button to turn it on. Tap it again to turn it off. Tap this button to change how loud the talking is."

Mos said, "Loud?"

Grenier nodded. He tapped his piece on and placed it in his right ear. The back wrap hooked nicely over his ear. He positioned the mike close to his mouth.

Mos did the same thing.

"Can you hear me?"

Mos ripped the piece away from his ear.

"That is loud. Tapped this button to make the noise softer."

Mos put the piece back on and tapped the volume button.

"How is this?" Grenier asked.

Mos had the volume down to 2. "Does not hurt.

Sound normal like you are next to me."

Grenier nodded. Quick study. "Alright everyone. Place your comm-pieces on and adjust the volume."

Kelly helped Oscar with his comm-piece.

The chimp grunted several times and moved his mouth like he was talking.

Steve scratched the top of his head.

"Now that we have been fed, can safely shot our weapons, and have communication here is what we are going to do." He looked around at the stern expressions around him. "We are outnumbered and out gunned. But we have the element of surprise on our side. The bad humans think we can't fight back. We can and we will. I'll make this plan simple. We shoot as many of them as we can. Go for the arms, stomach, and legs, please. Not the head."

Kiri asked, "Will they be dead?"

"If you shoot the head, yes. But we want them to fall asleep. That's what the bullets do. They are special bullets. The bad humans have to be punished. Killing them is not a punishment."

"Sleeping is not a punishment." Tutu responded.

"True, but when they wake up they will be put into a cage for a very long time. They will not be able to walk freely or see the sun or the moon. The cage is a little bigger than your shelter."

Hela and Feme gasped. "That is bad."

The proximity alarm went off.

Chapter 12

Codper stared at the cave entrance through binoculars. His Humvee was about 50 yards away hidden by several trees. He sent five soldiers to the cave opening as advance guard and another six to the back entrance. He knew there was a third entrance but it was unmarked. In passing some time ago, Grenier told him it was on top of a hill.

Grenier sat at the command station and checked the displays. Two soldiers slowly made their way to the front of the cave. Three soldiers can up to the rear entrance. None on the mountain top or the jungle entrance. He remembered telling the Colonel about the hill top entrance but not the one deep in the jungle. "Steve, Kelly, you two set?"

They both nodded.

Grenier turned to his small band of soldiers. "Remember, avoid head shots. Tutu, you lead. Steve and Kelly will be our eyes. They'll help as best they can from inside. Feme, you take the rear. Oscar you keep soldiers busy."

Oscar grinned teeth and signed, "Busy." He made a "B" with his right hand and bumped its wrist against the wrist of his left hand several times.

His Gemps. Grenier took a deep breath. His Gemps. Chances were good that they could come out of this alive. Though they had about two hours training they took to handling weapons and communication gear at a scary fast pace. Uncle Sam got his monies worth.

Codper watched as his advance guard disappeared through the cave entrance. His walkie-talkie crackled. "Entrance cleared." A minute later, "Rear entrance cleared."

Tutu stepped out of the exit first. It was a disguised rotting tree trunk centered amongst a cluster of tall leafy trees. One by one the Gemps slowly slipped out of the hole with Grenier taking up the rear. He had to improvise a LBE harness and belt for the Gemps at the last minute, but the look was impressive. They all wore goggled eye protection, a communications earpiece, the LBE and belt. They all held their weapons pointing to the ground, as instructed, trigger index finger on the barrel, safety on. Each Gemp demonstrated they could click the safety off, effortlessly, before squeezing the trigger.

Codper listened to the comm chatter. All doors accept one had the access code changed. Codper lifted the binoculars to his eyes and started scanning all the mountain tops. Oscar popped out of one. He checked his map. The chimp was about 60 yards from the cave entrance. He picked up his walkie-talkie. "Golf-one, mountain three, about 50 meters, chimp." He waited a second.

The walkie-talkie crackled, "Alpha-one, target spotted."

Codper watched, through his binoculars, Oscar rocking back and forth. Nasty beast he thought. Hope he hits you first shot. He counted to three when he saw the chimp flinch. He was so close.

A nearby rock exploded inches from Oscar's feet. The little chimp disappeared down the backside of the mountain. "Golf-one, maintain visual on spot. Shoot at your discretion, out."

Tutu signaled the other Gemps to fan out. Mos and Kiri took right with Hela and Feme taking left. Grenier checked their six. He heard Steve's voice of the comm. "Bad guys about 50 feet forward and left of G-1."

Tutu stopped and scanned the area toward his left. He saw movement crossing in front of him. He moved three steps to his left and saw a soldier walking toward the cave entrance. He heard a shot and paused.

Kelly said over the comm, "Miss. Sniper tried for Oscar."

Tutu took another step forward and to his left, clicked the gun off safe, and aimed. He controlled his breathing as Grenier instructed and squeezed the trigger. The gun barked loudly but the dart hit the mark.

The soldier's right arm jerked wildly away from his body. A second later he collapsed.

Tutu smiled. A flood of hormones hit the young Gemp. He had a hard-on.

Codper heard several shots. All of which did not sound like M16 rounds. He clicked the walkie-talkie talk button several times. "All teams, report in."

"Team six." Crackled in.

"Team 10." Came next.

"Team five."

"Team . . ." A gun barked through the tiny speakers.

Codper said, "Fuck!" He pulled his sidearm out and stepped away from the Humvee.

Grenier made his way to an area that had a good vantage point. He spotted two soldiers hiding in the foliage. Amateurs he thought as he aimed his pistol and barked out a round for each. Grenier moved further into the bush. He checked his six and saw movement. He was being shadowed. Stepping to the right he squatted down behind a tree. His shadow stopped a moment then moved to the left. He heard, "G-0, I'm to your left." He peeked around the tree and saw Mos with Kiri moving toward the Humvee. "Roger that. I see you."

Mos spotted Grenier first. He signed to Kiri, "Over there, G-0."

She nodded and followed Mos.

Both had been about twenty feet from Grenier when they saw him aim his pistol and double tap his trigger. He moved another six feet when he stopped for several seconds. He looked back and darted behind a tree. The two moved left of his position and transmitted they were near.

Kiri noticed that Grenier let out a slight sigh.

Oscar scampered down the side of the mountain after a small rock exploded near his feet. He made his way to the jungle floor and worked his way to the Humvee. He never liked the Colonel. Steve said he could bite him now and that was what he was going to do. A real nasty bite. One that would show blood, maybe bone. Oscar was happy with that thought. Very happy.

Codper thought he heard a twig snap. Two more teams stopped reporting and now he was worried.

Oscar had worked his way through the jungle around the long way to the Humvee. He could smell the Colonel's fear. It was thick and sour.

Codper turned around and saw the little chimp seconds before it leaped at him.

Tutu had taken out several other soldiers. The thrill of hunting Humans was almost too much. It was like a high he had never felt before. It was better than sex and the buildup was unbelievable.

Grenier had followed Mos and Kiri. Intuitively, the Gemps understood that Codper was the head of the snake. They moved through the jungle bush quickly, almost like they were borne from the land. It was uncanny he thought. Hours ago they feared God. Now they instilled the fear of God. If only he had the Gemps during Iraq and Afghanistan.

Mos and Kiri moved quickly through the bush. Grenier was behind them, but at a distance. Mos knew the human was capable of keeping up at this pace. Any faster and he would be further behind, out of sight. As Mos gave a quick side glance to Kiri he heard Steve's voice over the radio.

"Oscar just jumped the Colonel . . ."

Then he heard a distant gunshot.

"Oscar's down," Steve said. "Don't know how bad. Someone hurry!"

Tutu heard the shot and picked up his pace. The Elder down he thought. The bad human was going to hurt for this one.

Mos emerged from the jungle line in time to see Tutu on the other side of the Humvee. Codper had his left hand over what was left of his ear. His entire left side bloodied with a remnant of the ear exposed. Oscar bite through the cartilage and for that Codper shot him.

Codper screamed, "You fuckin' Monkey!

Oscar slowly got up holding his right arm. It was a flesh wound but deep enough to matter. He hissed at the

Colonel.

Codper aimed his pistol. This time he thought, this time you die you piece of shit goddamn fuckin' little beast. I hate you.

Tutu aimed his pistol and squeezed off a round. Grenier said no headshots. Tutu didn't obey.

The round struck Codper just behind the right ear. It shattered and knocked Codper to the ground unconscious. Unfortunately, the slow velocity bullet hit bone and disintegrated without penetrating. Codper would live.

Grenier wished he had been faster. When he entered the clearing it had already been too late. Codper was face down in the dirt. He walked over and felt for a pulse. The bastard was still alive. Pity. He resisted the urge to double tap some rounds into the back of his head, but the bastard needed to face military justice. He needed to spend life in a prison making big rocks out of little rocks until the day his ghost left his miserable pathetic hypocritical body. So much pain and suffering this one man caused. All for a belief. Grenier did what he thought a fitting punishment on his part. He spat in the Colonel's unconscious face. "Bastard," he said, backed up ten feet from the Colonel and shot him in the leg. He then picked up the walkie-talkie. "This is Colonel Grenier. Lieutenant Colonel Codper has been incapacitated. A Seal team has been dispatched to assist us and will arrive soon. You get one chance to surrender. This is it. I will not be making a second offer. Colonel out." He placed the walkie-talkie in his pocket and turned around. His Gemps had assembled around him. Oscar was between Hela and Feme. They were smoothing his head and making him feel better. Grenier's Gemps he thought. God help this world now.

The End

GEMP

ABOUT THE AUTHOR

J Carrell Jones studies people. His major in college was Anthropology before switching over to Computer Science and Information Technology. He worked in the Customer Support Services for many years, which gave him more opportunity in putting his understanding about people to good practical use. As a US Army veteran, he knows how to play hard and work tough. Nowadays, he gets his greatest joys in life by raising his brilliant young daughter, and writing.He lives in Southern California where the weather is mostly great with his wife, daughter, female cat, and three female Guinea pigs.

GEMP

www.ingramcontent.com/pod-product-compliance
Lightning Source LLC
Chambersburg PA
CBHW071828190726
48292CB00005B/1667